MY

BROTHER,

FATHER

...AND ME

MY SON'S WIFE SERIES

My Brother, Father...And Me
© Copyright 2018 Shelia E. Bell

ISBN: 978-1-944643-11-9

Library of Congress Control Number: 2018903445

His Pen Publishing, LLC
www.hispenpublishing.com

Cover designed by The Final Wrap
www.thefinalwrap.com

MY BROTHER,

FATHER

...AND ME

Shelia E. Bell

www.hispenpublishing.com

Douglasville, Georgia

More Titles by Shelia Bell
*Some titles are under former name of Shelia E. Lipsey

Young Adult Titles
House of Cars
The Life of Payne
The Lollipop Girl
The Righteous Brothers (Winter 2018)

Standalone Novels

Show A Little Love (out of print)
Always Now and Forever Love Hurts
Into Each Life
Sinsatiable
What's Blood Got To Do With It?
Only In My Dreams
The House Husband
Cross Road (Summer 2018)
Forever Ain't Enough (Summer 2018)
If the Price is Right (Winter 2018)
You Are Not the Bride (Winter 2018)
The Truth About Sista Brianna (Winter 2018)
On the 8th Day (Winter 2018)
Calling Dr. Daniel (Winter 2018)
The Couple (Fall 2018)
Christian Black, CEO (Winter 2018)
Ruthless Rianna (Summer 2018)
Love Shoulda Brought You Home (Summer 2018)

Series Books

Beautiful Ugly
True Beauty (sequel to Beautiful Ugly)

My Son's Wife Series
My Son's Wife
My Son's Ex-Wife: The Aftermath
My Son's Next Wife
My Sister My Momma My Wife
My Wife My Baby...And Him
The McCoys of Holy Rock
Dem McCoy Boys
My Brother, Father...And Me
Those Folks at Holy Rock

Adverse City Series
The Real Housewives of Adverse City
The Real Housewives of Adverse City 2
The Real Housewives of Adverse City 3
The Real Housewives of Adverse City 4

<u>Anthologies</u>
Bended Knees
Weary to Will
Learning to Love Me

<u>Nonfiction</u>
A Christian's Perspective: Journey Through Grief
How to Life Your Life Like It's Golden

<u>Titles written under Pseudonym K. C. Steele</u>
Scarlet's Sin
Scarlet's Redemption
Flawless Faith

Keep looking up...
That's the secret
of life...

Snoopy

Chapter 1

"He who angers you conquers you." Elizabeth Kenny

Hezekiah McCoy sat in his wheelchair ferociously contemplating his next move. George had received his sentencing and had reported to prison for a twenty-four month stint, if that long, leaving Hezekiah mostly in Detria's hands for his care and well-being. He was glad he had George take him to the bank before his shyster friend and blackmailer left to spend time with the young boys he so desperately craved when he was a free man. Maybe he would get a real wake up call, Hezekiah surmised, as he thought about George and his sick obsession.

Hezekiah withdrew his money and placed it in several other banks and money market accounts. It was close to a hundred thousand dollars, the same amount that was inside the walls of the condo he had, thanks to Holy Rock, before his traitor son changed the locks.

Again, Hezekiah put George on the case. George hired a shady locksmith who was able to pick the lock and give George and Hezekiah access to the condo one last time, only for Hezekiah to discover all of his money was gone! He was in a total uproar. If he could exact vengeance on the one who he knew stole it, Khalil McCoy, his eldest son, the boy would have been dead. Son or no son, Hezekiah would

have laid him out like Marvin Gaye's daddy did Marvin.
He would be looking up to heaven from whence cometh
his help. He could have very easily gotten George to hire
someone to off Khalil, but Hezekiah had other plans.

Whereas he was still tied down to a wheelchair and
unable to walk, he had regained some of his speech and
most of the time people could understand what he was
saying.

"Give me back my money, you conniving, sneaky,
thief!" he screamed into the phone as loud as his still weak
voice would allow.

Khalil, on the other end, laughed heartily. "Hey, Pops.
It's good to hear from you, too. It's been a minute, hasn't
it?"

"I want my money," Hezekiah seethed.

"I don't know what you're talking about. Then again,
let me think. Oh, could you possibly be referring to the 100
grand that was put away in that safe inside Holy Rock's
condo? Ummm, if that's what you're talking about, I say
finders keepers…losers weepers. By the way, you have no
proof that money, that is, if I actually found it, belongs to
you. I say if anything, it belongs to Holy Rock."

"You betta return my money…every penny of it,"
Hezekiah cursed and demanded as much as he could get
the words out.

"Look, Pops, it's been nice talkin' to ya, but I gotta go.
It's time for Bible study and I have a full house. You should
stop by sometime and hear the word of God, man. See ya."
Khalil hung up the phone, leaned back in his office chair,
clasped his hands together, and smiled.

If his father thought for one minute that he was about to
turn over the money he'd found, then he was crazier than

Khalil claimed he was after having had the stroke. No way would he ever tell anyone about the stash he'd found. He had thought for a brief moment about turning it over to the authorities so it could be returned to Holy Rock, but he decided against that idea. There was no way he could actually prove how much his father had embezzled, or if the money came from other sources Khalil was yet to discover.

He looked over his notes for this evening's midweek message, then put them aside and picked up the office phone. He picked up his cell phone and searched for the number to Memphis Police Department. When he found it, he dialed the number on his office phone.

"This is Pastor Khalil McCoy, senior pastor of Holy Rock Church. Will you connect me to someone who can help me? I'd like to report a crime of embezzlement."

Hezekiah was beside himself. How dare Khalil talk to him like he was some fool on the street. He showed no respect and then he all but boasted and admitted that he had taken Hezekiah's stash. It was times like this that he truly wished George was around, but that wasn't the case and it wouldn't be for quite some time. He had to learn how to make things happen on his own like he wasn't trapped in a wheelchair with extremely limited mobility. He rolled around in the small space of his room at the assisted living facility.

"Detria, I need to see you," Hezekiah practically yelled into the phone, obviously taking his frustration with Khalil out on her.

"Hold up, what's with the attitude? Good evening to you, too," she said sarcastically.

"I need you to come over here now," he said again, ignoring her reply to the manner in which he spoke.

"Uh, it's seven o'clock at night and I'm busy, Hezekiah. I won't be able to come tonight. Maybe tomorrow or the day after. I do have a life outside of you wanting me to be at your every beck and call, you know," she snapped.

"I said get over here now, or you'll be sorry," he ordered.

"Ughhh, I'm sick of you and all of your threats and demands." She paused momentarily and then said, "I'll be there as soon as I can."

Hezekiah ended the call abruptly and then proceeded to call another number saved into his phone.

Detria huffed and puffed while she stopped getting high, and then proceeded to get dressed. She called Priscilla on her cell phone and asked her to drive her to where Hezekiah was so she could see what he was up to now. She was literally fed up with being pushed around. It was equivalent to a form of abuse because when he wanted something, he would stop at nothing to get it. If she got up close enough to him, though he was in a wheelchair, he would slap her or hit her. His threats of doing something dangerous to her if she didn't abide by what he said kept her nervous and afraid. She thought she could relax her feelings of fear now that George was locked away and Hezekiah was limited on who he had to carry out his dastardly deeds, but it wasn't like that. She was still allowing him to manipulate her, but enough was enough. It was time she put an end to her jumping up and running to see what he wanted. Her sights were set on doing whatever she could to become Mrs. Khalil McCoy, First Lady of Holy Rock. That would take up all of her time.

"Are you ready?" Priscilla asked, jerking Detria from her thoughts.

"Yes, let's go. I want to get this over with." She sighed and waltzed out the door with Priscilla trailing behind.

"How's the kid?" Hezekiah asked the woman on the other end of the phone.

"He's good. How long are you going to be in that place? We haven't seen you since before you had the stroke," the woman said.

"You don't need to see me. As long as you're getting some change every month then you should be fine. Just stay away from me unless I say different. Understood?"

"Yeah," she said, sounding like a timid, submissive young girl.

"You still go to church?"

"Uh, no. Not really." Her voice was mild mannered and soft. Besides the woman who he had a kid with, Isabella was his next best-kept secret. Isabella had a kid too, which wasn't his, but Hezekiah made sure they were provided for as long as she remained loyal. He put her up in a two-bedroom bungalow in Arlington. He kept her quiet by threatening to put her back out on the streets.

She was homeless, barely a teen, when Hezekiah first encountered her through the homeless ministry Holy Rock ran. Three times a week a crew, which included Hezekiah, combed the streets of Memphis witnessing to the homeless. They carried them prepared foods, toiletries, clothing, blankets, and anything else they felt these individuals needed.

When he saw Isabella, he immediately felt a tug at his heart. The girl was skinny, frail, and all alone on the streets.

Despite her frail state, she was still beautiful. She looked like she was of Indian descent with long scraggly coal black hair, soft buttercream but pale colored skin and dark eyes. She told them with some reservation at first that she had no parents and had been on the streets since she was eleven years old. She told them she was eighteen, but Hezekiah didn't believe it. He guessed she was more like fourteen or fifteen.

Isabella wandered to Memphis a few months prior to the day Hezekiah and his team ran into her. Hezekiah couldn't leave her on the streets. He didn't want to leave any homeless person on the street, but such is life, and that was the reason he started the homeless ministry. If he couldn't rescue every homeless person, at least he could get Holy Rock involved in doing something for these people who had fallen on hard times. He understood most people were just a paycheck or two away from being homeless and that it could happen to anyone. He hadn't always been blessed to have money and he was far from being rich, but he had found his calling in the ministry and it had treated him well.

Hezekiah put her up in a motel. He continued to pay for her to remain at the motel and would visit her often. He soon discovered she was not exactly innocent as she acted. On one of his weekly visits, he saw a man exiting her motel room. He was shocked and angry. He took her for an innocent young girl but he later discovered she was getting money by prostituting, and she was using the room Holy Rock was paying for to turn her tricks.

When he confronted her about it, she confessed that she had been a prostitute for as long as she had been on the streets. She was from Canton, Ohio and had migrated to Memphis via stowing away on trains, hitchhiking, and doing whatever necessary to find money and keep her belly filled.

Hezekiah told her if she expected him to continue to keep a roof over her head she had to promise him she would stop prostituting herself. The girl agreed, but weeks later, when Hezekiah saw her belly growing bigger, he realized it wasn't from eating too much. He made sure she was well fed but food wasn't what was causing her weight gain. Hezekiah wasn't a doctor but he suspected she had a brat in her belly.

The girl confirmed that she was pregnant and didn't know who the father was. Hezekiah got her some medical attention, put her up in a small apartment, and the girl started attending Holy Rock. Their relationship took a major turn when Hezekiah came to the apartment one evening to check on her. Shortly after he arrived, they were laughing, talking, and watching movies, which they sometimes did. He fell asleep on the sofa and awoke to the girl lying underneath his arm, curled up and sleeping as well. He pushed the hair back off her face and stared down at her. She was beautiful. He looked at her swollen belly, and then kissed her on the top of her head. He was no better than George in a way because he liked them young, and Isabella fit the definition of young, beautiful and she was experienced.

The teen woke up, looked up into Hezekiah's eyes, and then pulled herself up until she was positioned on top of him. Day turned into afternoon. Afternoon turned into evening as Hezekiah gave his flesh everything it wanted.

Chapter 2

"Anger is a wind which blows out the lamp of the mind."
Robert Ingersoll

Fancy opened the priority express envelope. Tears flooded her eyes and she placed a hand over her mouth as she read its contents.

You have fourteen days from the receipt of this letter to get out of my house. No exceptions, no extensions. The house has been officially sold to a private buyer. You thought you could destroy me, hurt me, and kick me to the curb. You should have known better, Fancy. I thought we had something that would last a lifetime, but you proved that wasn't the case. I loved you. I tried to make you happy and give you everything a woman like you could possibly want. But it wasn't enough. You made that clear when you turned your back on me after I had the stroke. You don't have to worry about seeing a lawyer. My lawyer's business card is included in this letter. You will see I have already filed divorce proceedings. You and my sons have turned out to be a huge disappointment. Everything I've done for you only to be treated like I'm nothing. I guarantee this though, Fancy, you reap what you sow. Karma is real, baby. Believe that. The letter was signed, *Once the love of your life, Hezekiah.*

Fancy collapsed on the sofa in the family room and wept. How could he do this? What happened to the love they once shared? They had been through so much together, all for it to come down to this? She still loved Hezekiah, no matter how much he believed she didn't. He was the one who had wronged her, but now he had turned things around to make it appear all that happened between them was her fault. It wasn't. She pulled out the business card. Minutes later, as if by design, the doorbell rang. Fancy got up and slowly walked to the door. She opened it and saw a sheriff.

"Yes," she said humbly. "How can I help you?"

"I'm looking for a...uh," he looked at the paper he held in his hand, "Fancy McCoy."

"I'm Mrs. McCoy. What is it?"

"You've been served, ma'am." He pushed the envelope into her hands, tipped his sheriff hat, and then turned around and left.

Fancy opened the envelope while standing in the doorway. When she opened it, she saw the official copies of divorce papers Hezekiah had filed for "irreconcilable differences."

She remained in the open doorway while she cried. All the years she and Hezekiah had been together...since they were teens, had come down to this. He was divorcing her and throwing her out of the house they had shared since he became senior pastor of Holy Rock. Granted, the boys had taken her side against their father, but how could Hezekiah blame them for that? He was the one who had cheated. He was the one who had stolen from the church. He was the one who physically tried to run her down in his chair. He was the one who had betrayed her with God knows who this woman was that sent her that Will in the mail. So how could he blame her for the demise of their marriage?

Fancy was heartbroken. She felt all alone. She had no true friends she could call on. Her life and world revolved around Hezekiah, and she didn't trust other women. She finally closed the door, turned around, and walked back into the family room where she retrieved the first envelope she had received earlier. She picked it up, walked along the hallway, and went upstairs to her bedroom. Throwing the papers haphazardly on the nearby night table, Fancy flung herself on her bed and continued sobbing.

Chapter 3

"Men can starve from a lack of self-realization as much as they can from a lack of bread." Richard Wright

Xavier and Ian returned from a three-day weekend getaway to New Orleans. He needed time away from family and all the drama going on at Holy Rock and between his parents. With his dreams of attending Xavier dashed for now, he made the trip to enjoy himself in the New Orleans French Quarter. He invited Ian to come along and they had a great time. They had much in common and Xavier found Eliana's brother easy to talk to and to hang with, except Ian could act a little too flamboyant at times for Xavier's taste. Nevertheless, he tried to ignore that about Ian's personality and chose to concentrate on the good times he enjoyed with him.

Before taking the train to New Orleans, the two of them had spent most of their free time together since they met at Eliana's house a few months back. Their relationship was innocent and until they arrived in New Orleans, they considered themselves platonic friends. All of that changed the second morning they were there. Since that time, they had become lovers and Xavier couldn't be happier. He thought there would never be anyone who could make him happy, make him smile, or make him feel the way

Raymone had made him feel, but boy had he been wrong. He still thought about Raymone, and occasionally tried to reach out to him via email, but never received a response. Raymone no longer had the same cell phone number, had deleted his social media accounts, and it was as if he never existed. It weighed on Xavier heavily at times because he was the reason for Raymone's permanent disability of living as a quadriplegic. He prayed time and time again to God for forgiveness, but for Xavier it never seemed to be quite enough. He felt so guilty, so horrible about the accident. Was it because he was a gay man that he was being subjected to these awful feelings? Was God getting back at him for the lifestyle he lived? He tormented himself constantly because he didn't want to be the way he was. He didn't want to succumb to the desire he had for other men, but it was like he was an addict. It was as if he was addicted to living this often persecuted lifestyle.

Now that he had met Ian, he struggled even more with his sexuality. One part of him adored the relationship he and Ian were developing and the other part of him was in a mental struggle for him choosing to lie with a man and not a woman.

"Hey, we have to do this again," Ian said as they walked to the Memphis Central Station parking garage where they had parked and left their cars.

"Yeah, we do. I had a great time," Xavier said, "but now it's back to work. I'm sure there's plenty of drama I've luckily missed out on since being out of the M-town."

Ian laughed as they continued the short trek to their individual cars parked next to each other.

"Well, thanks for inviting me to go with you," said Ian.

"You bet. I'm glad you accepted." They arrived at their

cars and stood in between the two vehicles. "Since, uh, since things went to the next level, where do we stand, in your opinion?" Xavier asked. He didn't want to appear too forward or act like he expected anything to be different, but inside he hoped they would get closer.

"I say we take it one day at a time. I really like you. I like you a lot, and of course I still want to see you. But you told me you're still dealing with some issues about your friend who was horribly injured. You feel it's your fault, and you said yourself you don't know if you've gotten over him completely. I wouldn't want to push you into anything, Xavier. Just because we... well just because things turned up in New Orleans, I don't expect anything from you other than friendship. And you told me too that you're wrestling with your homosexuality. Unlike you, I'm in a good place. If God doesn't accept me the way I am, then I figure it's his loss, you know."

Xavier nodded, not in agreement per say but because he was listening, really listening to every word Ian spoke. He wished he could be as carefree and not give a darn what others thought but he wasn't like that. He cared what people thought and what they said behind his back. He wasn't as strong and secure in who he was like Ian.

"I won't live my life like I'm a mistake," Ian continued. "I am who I am. If anybody doesn't like it then that's on them, and not me. I believe in God and from what I've been taught, he made us. He knows everything about me and about you, Xavier. Do you think us being homosexual escaped him when he was the one who formed us? It says he knew us before we were formed in our mother's wombs. What does that say about him?"

Xavier looked at Ian curiously. He had never heard it

put quite like that before regarding his homosexuality. If God made him, knew him before he was formed, ordained every day of his life, then surely God knew his lifestyle. What Ian said made so much sense. He had a lot to think about. Thanks to Ian, he could look at things in his life differently. If his brother, his mother, or his wayward father didn't approve of him and his choices, that would be their problem and not his. That's what he momentarily told himself. Whether he could actually begin to see things like Ian, he didn't know, but he was sure going to give it a try.

The two of them embraced and said their goodbyes. "I'll talk to you later," Ian said.

"Yeah, maybe we'll hook up tomorrow, have dinner, or something. I want to check out the new super hero movie that came out this past weekend. You up for it?"

"Sure, just text me or give me a call. I'm going back to work tomorrow but we'll talk later tonight."

They embraced once again, then opened the door to their respective cars and got inside. They waved at each other as they started their cars and drove off.

Xavier exhaled, smiled, and then went into deep thought as he replayed the conversation he and Ian had. He had to stop being so hard on himself. If he was going to live this lifestyle, he had to learn to be okay with it. He didn't want to run from his problems any longer. Yes, he still had plans to go away or maybe stay in Memphis and attend college. People did it everyday—attended school online. He planned to look into doing just that. Ian opened his eyes and his mind to a lot of things. Ian was smart, intelligent, funny, and successful. He attended college while working a full time job and he still made time to do many of the things he loved.

Xavier thought about it more and came to the conclusion that he could do what needed to be done at Holy Rock, go to college, and still live his life the way he wanted to live it. He told himself he would no longer be under the rules and decisions of others, including his parents and his brother. He was not going to hide who he truly was…that was his intent. He prayed he could pull it off.

Chapter 4

"All good things must come to an end." H.H. Riley

Xavier arrived at home and all was rather quiet. The house was dark. He didn't sense life anywhere. He stopped in the kitchen, opened the refrigerator, and got himself a bottled water and made two hoagie sandwiches out of some shredded barbeque chicken he saw in the fridge. He piled both sandwiches with chicken, lettuce, tomatoes, onions, and lots of mayo, his favorite condiment, followed by a sprinkle of pepper before topping it with the top parts of the giant size hoagie buns.

Next, he looked inside the kitchen pantry and moved around some bags of tortilla chips, popcorn, and cookies until he found a bag of potato chips. He got the bag of chips and took his sandwiches and water upstairs to his bedroom.

That was another thing he thought about as he walked up the stairs. He was a grown man. He needed his own spot. He could afford it now that he was on Holy Rock's payroll, and making a darn good salary.

As he walked past his mother's room, he saw the door cracked. He walked over and peeped inside and saw her lying across the bed. He tapped lightly on the door. "Mom, you awake?"

Fancy quickly raised her head. "Xavier, honey. You're back. Did you have a good time?"

"Yea, I did. I needed that break. New Orleans is the bomb," he said, laughing lightly.

Fancy sat up and then got up off the bed, hoping her baby boy wouldn't notice her red swollen eyes, but that was not the case.

"Mom, what's wrong? Have you been crying?" He walked all the way into her room until he stood in front of her. "What happened? What has Dad done now?" He knew that had to be the reason for her tears. His father was practically the only person on earth he knew of who could make her cry.

"It...it's nothing. At least nothing me and the good Lord can't handle."

"Tell me what it is. I know it has to be something involving my father."

"I don't want to bother you with me and your father's problems, Xavier. You and Khalil have already been through enough dealing with that man and his foolishness."

"Tell me, Ma," Xavier insisted.

"I…we…have to move. Your father sold the house to a private buyer. We have two weeks to be out of here."

"That's low. I can't believe he would do something like this. It was bad enough when he had the lights turned off and stopped paying the mortgage, but to throw you out, that's foul, even for him."

Fancy began crying again. This time her tears came slowly. She wiped them away as quickly as they fell. "I should have listened to your brother when he first told me to find a place of my own. I went looking but I guess I just couldn't let this place go. Now I don't have a choice."

"Ma, it's going to be all right." Xavier wanted to console her so he placed his plate of food, chips, and bottled water on the bed, and then he gathered his mother into his arms and held her while she cried. "Lately, I've been thinking that it's time for me to get my own place anyway. And you, well, finding you another spot will be easy. There are lots of folks at Holy Rock who sell real estate, manage apartment complexes, and rent houses, the whole nine yards. We'll find you a nice crib in no time. Don't you worry, Ma. Don't you worry about a thing."

Fancy pulled away from her son's arms, stood on tiptoes, and kissed him on his cheek.

"Thank you, son. I know everything will work out. It's just a hard pill to swallow. So many memories have been made in this house and now to think that your father has sold it, and he doesn't want to be married to me anymore, it's tough to think about."

"What do you mean he doesn't want to be married to you anymore? What would make you say that? I know Dad has put you through a whole lot, but in the end, I guess I thought you two would eventually work things out. You always do. You've said it yourself. You and dad have been through some troubling times during all the years you've been together, but you persevered and made it through them all. What makes you think that once he gets better, and clears his mind, that he won't ask for your forgiveness and try to rectify the things he's done. Don't you want that?"

"He's done so much this go round, sweetheart. I don't think our marriage can be salvaged, and even if I had hoped it could, your father doesn't feel the same." She turned around, leaned down, and picked up the brown envelope and gave it to Xavier. This is what came today, delivered by

a sheriff I should add, along with a priority mail package
about us having to move.

Xavier scanned the papers, looked up at his mother,
and a frown caused a deep crease in his forehead. "What is
wrong with him, Ma? He's nothing like the father I grew up
with. I'm sorry. That's all I can say." His voice was tender
and sad.

Fancy reached up and brought his head down to her
shoulder. "It's all right, Xavier. Like you said, I'm going
to be fine. We're going to be fine. God has a reason for all
of this. I just have to trust that He will handle it. Now, go
on and eat your food. I just grilled that chicken last night.
Your brother came over and had dinner with me. He said it
was good," Fancy said, trying to smile and talk through her
pain.

"I know it's going to be good. I love your barbeque
chicken."

"You love anything I cook," she said, patting him on his
back as he leaned down and picked up his food and bottled
water.

Xavier cracked a smile. "Get some rest, Ma. If you need
me, holla."

Xavier walked back toward the open bedroom door.

"Oh, son," Fancy said. "We have to talk about you
moving into your own place. Don't think I let that fly over
my head. I don't see why you feel you need to be out on
your own. I love having you with me."

"Ma, I'm not a kid anymore. I need my own space, a
place I can call my own. I don't want to be living with my
momma. That's meant as no offense to you. I'm just saying,
it's not cool."

Fancy waved a hand toward him. "Go on so you can eat.

We'll talk about it later. Goodnight, Zay."

Goodnight, Ma. And promise me you won't worry. First thing tomorrow, we'll start looking for a place for you… and for me. Have you told Khalil?"

"Not yet. I guess I'll call him now. Goodnight."

"Gnite, Ma." Xavier exited the room, closing the door behind him. He was angrier than he cared to show at his father's latest antics. What had gotten into that man? He used to have the utmost respect for his father when he was growing up. He thought he was the equivalent to some of the strong black men he read about and admired so much, but seeing how things were going in his family, Xavier lost respect for his dad and looked at him in a totally different light. He shook his head as he walked toward his room. His father had literally evicted his mother out of the house she called her dream home. What a shame.

Xavier opened his bedroom door with one hand while balancing his food in the other when his text notifier sounded. He kicked the door closed with his foot, then set his food on the nearby desk in his exceptionally large bedroom. He eyed the text message as he set the phone down next to his food.

It was a message from Ian. You made it to the crib?

Xavier smiled and then texted back. Yea. Bout to eat something. You good?

Yeah, I'm straight. Just checkin with you. Still thinking about NOLA.

Me too. It was better than I could've ever expected, Xavier replied, thinking about the experience he had with Ian.

Go on and eat. I'm bout to do the same

then I'm crashing. Ttyl.

GN ttyl, Xavier texted back, laid his phone down, and exchanged it for his plate of food that was now cold. He picked up the plate and ran back downstairs, rewarmed it in the microwave, and then raced back up the stairs where he sat at the desk and devoured the meal.

Chapter 5

"Nothing remains constant except change itself." Unknown

Stiles sat behind his desk in his office at Full of Grace Ministries, still feeling shocked about Khalil's offer to him to return to Holy Rock. Could he do it? Did he even *want* to return to the church and how would it affect his ministry at Full of Grace? There was a time when he would have given anything to grace that pulpit again but now he wasn't so sure. He had to pray, really seek God's guidance and direction before he gave Khalil his answer.

Khalil told him to take his time, think about it, and then get back to him. Stiles made up his mind to do exactly that.

Knock, knock.

"Come in."

Kareena walked in, looking lovely as ever. Her hair was in long thick locks that cascaded past her shoulders and down her back. Her dark skin was such a turn on for Stiles. And her walk…her walk was like someone walking on clouds. She was just that light on her feet, and every move was like a sleek gazelle. Her thick lips were soft as cotton. He knew that because he had the pleasure of feeling them against his many times. Her tiny waist, petite frame, and luscious bottom sent lustful chills up and down his spine and saturated his mind with thoughts that a Godly man like himself shouldn't have been having, but he did.

"Morning, Kareena."

"Good morning, Pastor Graham. It's time to go over the membership reports. Are you ready?"

"As ready as I'm ever going to be. Let's do this. Pull out a chair and sit down."

For the next hour and forty minutes, they went through the membership roll. When they were done, Stiles invited her to have lunch.

"You want to go somewhere to have a sandwich or would you like to have a full course meal? Your choice?" he offered.

"I *am* hungry. I didn't eat breakfast, so I can use some real food." Kareena and Stiles laughed.

He loved this about Kareena. She was not afraid to be herself. She was funny and carefree about life, and enjoyed the simpler things, yet she could be spontaneous. On top of that, she was smart and there was nothing she didn't know about her father's church, Full of Grace. When he died, and Stiles began leading the church, it was Kareena who helped him maneuver through the day-to-day functions, ministries, and staff. She was a whiz at it all and he was grateful for her.

Stiles stood up and walked from behind his desk, while Kareena stood too.

"I'm going to go and put these in my office," she said. "I'll meet you outside. Your car or mine?"

"Mine," Stiles said. "Unless you insist on chauffeuring me today," he teased.

"Me? Chauffeur you? Not in this lifetime," she mocked.

Stiles chuckled and they walked up the hallway. She

stopped in her office along the way and Stiles proceeded to the side door leading to a small, covered, two car private parking area.

Minutes later, Kareena appeared. He looked at her in awe again. The blue, sleeveless, v neckline dress she wore had what was called a handkerchief hem and empire waist. It rested just above her knees, showcasing her beautiful, shapely legs. He swallowed hard as he stood next to the passenger door with it opened, allowing her access into his ride.

"Ready?"

"Yep. I'm ready and I'm starving," she said and reared her head back and laughed.

As usual, they enjoyed talking and laughing while they ate. Things turned serious when Kareena posed a question.

"Have you given the offer to return to Holy Rock any more thought?"

Stiles shook his head from side to side, while chewing his food. He picked up a napkin from off the table, and wiped his mouth before responding verbally.

"I'm seeking God. As much as I would like to accept the offer, I can't, in good conscious, forsake my duties at Full of Grace Ministries. Khalil said he would not require me to be there but one, maybe two, Sundays a month. They would fly me in or pay for my transportation if I drove. I would be expected to fill in when my nephew is on sabbatical or called away."

"That could be worked out at Full of Grace. All you need to do is find a good assistant pastor, or have guest ministers come in and preach during your absence. I mean, at the end of the day, you have to do what you feel is right for you, Stiles. I know how much Holy Rock meant to you and how much it still means."

Kareena reached across the table and kneaded Stiles' hand in hers. "You know inside your heart what direction you want to take. I think I know you well enough to know that about you." She smiled tenderly at him, removed her hand, and then proceeded to finish eating her meal.

"You're right when you said I need to do what's best for me, but it's bigger than that, Kareena. I have to operate under God's direction. I don't want this to become a 'me' thing. You know what I mean?"

"Yes, I understand. I'm just saying that you have a feeling about what you should do. Pray about it like you're doing. God will direct you."

They enjoyed the remainder of their meals and then returned to the church. The rest of the day went by relatively fast. Stiles went home, kicked back in his man cave, before getting on his knees and petitioning God for direction and answers.

When he finished praying, he made himself two sandwiches, opened a can of tomato soup, and proceeded to watch an ESPN sports talk show.

His phone rang in the middle of the program. He picked up the phone from the table and looked at it—it was Fancy.

"Hi, there," he said. "How's it going?"

It took a few seconds before she responded.

"Hello?" Stiles said again. "Fancy?"

"Hi, it's me. Were you busy?"

"No, just sitting here eating and watching television. What's up? Everything okay on the home front?"

"That's why I was calling." Fancy didn't want to break down over the phone, but she couldn't help it. She was so hurt about Hezekiah's latest actions. Having no one but her sons to confide in, she turned to the person outside of her sons and nearest to her, the one who she knew she could trust.

"Fancy? You sound like you're crying. What happened?"

"It's Hezekiah."

Stiles' heart pounded as he thought about what she was about to say. "Is...is he...is he dead?" Stiles asked, not wanting to hear the answer he felt she was about to give.

"No...thank God, it's nothing like that. I assume he's doing better but I haven't personally spoken to him or seen him in some time."

"Whew, I'm glad to hear my brother is alive. Thank God for that. I've been praying for him constantly. We still believe God for his healing. So tell me what happened?"

"I got a letter yesterday and I was served divorce papers. I have to be out of the house in two weeks. Hezekiah sold the house to some private buyer. He sent me a letter by priority express mail. After receiving the letter is when I was served with divorce papers."

"Oh, my God. I'm so sorry, Fancy. I don't know what's up with my brother. Have you found a place to live yet? When we went and looked at houses you couldn't narrow it down to one or even to your top three." Stiles laughed.

Fancy placed a hand over her mouth and laughed, too. "Yea, I know right, but that's because I thought I had time so I wasn't really giving it much thought. But things are different now, which is why Xavier and I went out looking earlier this morning. Khalil is lining up some places for me to look at, too. The blessing is we have some good real estate agents at the church that Khalil knows. He's reached out to one that he especially likes who's worked closely with several of the staff ministers in the past to help them with purchasing homes. In the meantime, a mover came over and helped me pack my things. I'm taking everything in this house, every stitch of furniture there is, and every pot, pan, fork and knife. I'm even taking the toilet tissue. And do you know he had the audacity to send someone over here about an hour ago to pack up the furniture and his clothes? Thank God, everything was moved out by that time. The nerve of him, Stiles. But I'm glad I had the mind to have the movers move everything out of that house. Serves him right."

"Where are you now?"

"I'm at a hotel. I couldn't stay at that house if I wanted to. It's not mine anymore. My dreams, my memories, all of it's gone. Khalil said I could stay with him until I found something, but I don't want to impose on him or anyone else. I can afford a hotel. I *am* on the church's payroll, so I'm making some money to take care of myself."

Stiles felt bad for Fancy. She was a wonderful woman. How could Hezekiah throw his marriage, his family to the side like that? Stiles couldn't understand the man's reasoning.

"Where is Xavier? He staying with you or is he with Khalil?"

"He's staying with one of his friends," she said and left it at that. She didn't want to think about where he was staying or God knows who he was staying with. She had enough on her plate and that was the last thing she wanted to dwell on.

"Do you have any idea if Hezekiah is still at the nursing facility?"

"No, he's in an assisted living facility, I think. At least, that's the last I heard."

"What did you do with all of your furniture? Put it in storage?"

"Yes, that's exactly what I did. I'll let it rot in there before I give him any of it. I have an appointment with an attorney that Khalil set me up with. She's a new member at Holy Rock. She's supposed to have a great reputation as a divorce attorney. We'll see. I will meet her tomorrow. All of this is weighing on me, Stiles. I hate to keep bombarding you with my worries, but right now, you're the only true friend I have."

"How many times do I have to remind you—I'm here for you. I mean that."

"I know you do, and I'm thankful for your friendship."

"Look, I'm praying for you. Keep me posted about your whereabouts and about the meeting with the attorney. And call me anytime. You hear me?"

"Yes, I hear you,"

"I mean it, Fancy," he reiterated.

"I know you do. Goodnight, Stiles."

They ended the call, and Fancy curled up in the hotel bed and flipped channels on the TV remote. She began thinking about the kiss she'd given Stiles. She couldn't deny that it ignited a fire inside her when she did it. It wasn't because Stiles was so good looking, although he was, but that wasn't what drew her to kiss him like she had. It was his self-assuredness, the way he carried himself, his swagger, it all exuded sex appeal and power, and it drove her wild. There was no way she would ever cross the line and try to pursue something more. She couldn't do that. It would be too degrading to her and to her ending marriage. Yet, she was not going to lie to herself either. She was attracted to him but that was that on that. She refused to let it be anything more. She had to remain in control of her feelings. There had never been another man, besides Hezekiah, in her life and until God totally closed the doors with him, she would keep her legs closed and her kisses to herself.

Chapter 6

"Trust, but verify." Ronald Reagan

"Where are you laying your head since Dad threw you and Mom out of the house?" Khalil asked his brother as they walked the treadmill at the gym.

"With a friend," Xavier responded without giving information about him sharing Ian's bed.

"I know this friend?"

"Maybe or maybe not. But what's it to you? Long as I have a place to lay my head."

"Look, bruh, I don't care where you lay your head, long as you're laying it somewhere safe. But you're a grown man, you know. You can handle your own spot right about now. You feel me?"

"Yeah, and I got one up on you. I already put in an application for my own spot. S'pose to hear something in a few days. I don't see why I wouldn't be approved though."

"Where is it?"

"The same complex where your girl lives."

"My girl? Who? Which one? I got several, you know." Khalil laughed as he turned up the treadmill a notch.

"I'm sure you do, but I'm talking about Eliana."

"Oh, now I see."

"What do you mean now you see?"

"First, don't try to make this about me. What you're saying is you want to be close to ole boy, huh? Look, bruh, you live your life the way you wanna. All I'm going to say about it is to be careful who you lay down next to and be careful who you let come up in your spot. You feel me?"

"Yeah, I do."

The brothers continued with their workout, something they did at least three times a week, though Khalil preferred to work out everyday.

They finished their workout, took showers, and then left the gym. Xavier drove off first, leaving Khalil behind talking to some girl he was pushing up on. He was a pastor, but he was still a woman thirsty man who loved flirting and testing the strength of his game with the ladies.

After he walked away and headed outside to his car, he was approached by a man who he noticed when he first walked outside into the night.

"Hey, man," the short, but muscular and bearded white guy said.

"What up?" Khalil said, detecting that the guy was up to no good. He could sense trouble from being on the streets himself for so many years. "What you need, potna?"

"You that pastor from Holy Rock?" the stranger asked.

"Yeah, I am. What can I do for you?" Khalil's radar was on full force. What did this dude want?

"I just wanted to tell you that I been to your church a few times. I thought that was you when I saw you in the gym. I enjoy your messages. You for real, for real," the stranger said.

"Thanks, man. What's your name?"

"Danny," he answered.

"Well, Danny, I'm glad you enjoy the services. I hope you become a member, but even if you don't, I hope you continue to attend the church."

"Yeah, I'll do that. See you, bruh."

Khalil extended his hand to the guy and they shook.

"Be safe," the guy said, and walked off.

Khalil got inside his ride and sped off the parking lot of the gym.

As he drove home, he thought about the television ministry he was working on. It would be broadcast live on Sunday mornings and again on Wednesday evenings during Bible Study. It was going to cost a pretty penny for him to have a live broadcast but he was going to find a way to fund the program with Holy Rock footing most of the bill, of course. He still had some out of pocket expenses that he needed covered and he already knew the perfect person to set out the funds. No way was he going to use any of the stash he found of his father's. That was for his own personal use. He had set up several bank accounts, spreading the money in increments of under ten thousand dollars so as not to be detected or raise suspicion. He also invested some of it in a money market account and a couple savings accounts that paid hefty interest.

Lately, he had been studying about the stock market, and he used another portion of the money to purchase stocks with the help of a financial advisor. He was definitely going to have that money working for him rather than having it stashed away behind a vent where it couldn't earn a dime. His father wasn't so smart after all.

He called Detria. She had long since stopped texting him like she was crazy, but instead he would receive a phone call or text from her every couple weeks. Khalil guessed

that she was trying to keep his mind on her but he mostly
ignored her. Now that the opportunity for the television
ministry was about to happen, it was time he talked to her.

"Hey, what's up?" he asked as she quickly answered the
phone.

"Khalil? What a surprise. How are you, baby?"

"I'm good, just missing you. Can I stop by? I got a
proposition for you."

"Uh, sure. I miss you. I'd love to see you. When will
you be here?" she asked.

"What? I'm on a time frame or something? It's like that
now?"

"No, of course, not. I just wanted to know so I could tell
Priscilla to be on the lookout for you. I'm upstairs. I'll be
waiting on you. Bye, sugar."

Khalil didn't reply. He ended the call and made the turn
that lead to Detria's crib.

Chapter 7

"I trust everyone. I just don't trust the devil inside them."
Troy Kennedy-Martin

"Do you really have to leave?" Detria asked as she watched Khalil climb out of her bed and proceed to dress.

"Yeah, I can't spend the night. I wanted to see you, talk to you about a couple of things."

"Yeah, you did say you had a proposition for me, but I thought you just gave it to me." Detria sat up in the bed and laughed.

"You got jokes, huh? Seriously, I do have something I want to run by you—see if you're interested."

"Okay, what is it?"

"I'm starting a televangelism ministry. The plan is for Holy Rock to broadcast live two days a week. I have most of the ends and outs of getting it off the ground already taken care of. The plan is to start production in about six weeks. I'm still looking for investors. Although Holy Rock will be footing most of the cost, it's pushing our budget to the max. That's where people like you come in."

"So that's the reason you're here? You need money? My money, specifically." Detria looked at him, waiting on a response. Inside, she thought *Whatever he needs, I'm going to give. If it'll keep him in my bed then the next step will be to convince him to put a ring on it.*

"You should know I don't hold back when it comes to speaking what's on my mind. Yeah, I need your money, Dee. Is that what you wanna hear? But I also like your honey," he said, flashing a smile at her as he finished buttoning his shirt. He then jumped back on the bed, gathered her into his arms, and began kissing her deeply.

When he pulled away, he said, "So, what's it going to be? You my secret partner or nah?" He kissed her again and touched her in all the right spots.

Detria could hardly speak. Her body betrayed her every time she was in Khalil McCoy's arms. "Yeees," she said between moans. "I'm in...all the way in."

Khalil drove home feeling satisfied that Detria bought in to the deal to help him with the television ministry. He practically grinned the entire time he drove to his apartment.

He pulled into his parking space, got out of the car, and proceeded to his upstairs apartment when he heard something behind him. He stopped, looked around, and that's when he saw him...the same guy from the gym.

"Hey, man, what's up?" Khalil said, sensing trouble.

"I think you have a debt to settle with a friend of ours. Seems like you got something of his," the guy said.

"Look, I don't know what you're talking about. I don't want any trouble, bruh. You go and tell whoever sent you they have the wrong brother."

Khalil moved a step closer toward his apartment, remaining cautious.

"I think I have the right man. Matter of fact, I know I do. Now we can do this the easy way or the let's say...the more difficult way."

Another man suddenly appeared and Khalil knew that

whatever was about to go down, it wasn't going to be pretty. He decided to make a run for it, and took off running away from his crib.

The two men chased him, but Khalil was fast. He learned how to run from the cops and his enemies at a young age. He ducked and dodged the two men until he didn't see or hear them behind him anymore. He looked around and found he had ran far from his apartment. He was actually near the strip that was lined with bars, restaurants, and quaint businesses. He walked inside one of the coffee shops, headed straight to their bathroom, went into one of the stalls, and plopped down—exhausted, but grateful to have escaped the two goons.

He sat on the toilet inside the stall for a while, contemplating his next move. He felt inside his pocket to see if he still had his phone. He didn't know if he had lost it in the midst of his run. He hadn't. He exhaled again, then called Omar to come and pick him up.

"I'll fill you in on what happened when you get here. Just get here as soon as you can."

"I'm on my way," Omar replied.

Khalil leaned back in the stall and replayed what had just happened around in his mind. Who could it have been that would want to bring him harm? It didn't take long before he realized just who that person was—Hezekiah McCoy. His own father wanted to bring harm, maybe even death. Things had just gotten real, seriously real, for Khalil. Hezekiah wanted his money, but he wasn't going to get it. Khalil was his father's son, and like Hezekiah, he wasn't going to be bullied, beaten, or threatened.

"You wanna play this game then game on, Pops. Game on."

"Thanks for coming, man. I owe you one," Khalil told Omar as he looked around before jumping inside Omar's car.

"You don't owe me nothing, bruh, except an explanation as to why you looking like you just got the scare of your life. You aite?"

"I'm good. Just got approached at my crib by these two dudes trying to rob me. I took off running, man. I wasn't about to lead them up to my crib or my ride. Thank God, I lost 'em."

"Man, for real? You get a good look at 'em?"

"Yeah. One of 'em came up to me outside the gym earlier this evening. Said he enjoyed my sermons. Said he'd been to Holy Rock a few times. You know, making small talk."

"That's weird, and then he followed you to the crib?"

"No, I don't think so 'cause I made a stop for a few hours before I went home. I don't know if they had been waiting on me all that time or not, but the thing is they knew where I lived and they obviously know who I am. Probably thought I had a grip, but I don't keep but a coupla hundred on me. You know what I mean?"

"Man, I'm glad you're safe. You gonna go back to the crib? You can always lay low at my place, you know. We can check out your crib when the sun comes up. I'll get strapped, too. We don't want nothing to go down unless we're both protected."

"Yeah, I hear you. My piece is at the crib. Khalil didn't carry a gun because of his past criminal history. If stopped by the cops he didn't want to chance anything unnecessary going down. His juvenile records were sealed, of course, but he was a black man driving, and after seeing what happened to Xavier a few months ago, and the experiences he gained from dealing with the police in Chicago, he knew what to do and what not to do.

"I think I'll take you up on your offer, at least for the night."

The following morning, bright and early, Omar drove Khalil back to his apartment. They checked out Khalil's ride first. The windows had all been broken and the car ransacked. Khalil bit his bottom lip. He was furious.

"Man, this seems more than an attempted robbery gone bad. Looks like they were gunning for you for some reason or other. Like you got on the bad side of one of them chicks you be messing with," Omar joked but sounded serious at the same time. "Or maybe her man got wind of you."

Khalil was too hot to respond. He dashed off toward his apartment. He searched for his keys inside his pocket but he didn't have them. He remembered he had them in his hand when he took off running. He must have dropped them. He went to the door, but didn't have to open it because it was already slightly ajar. Omar pulled his piece out while Khalil kicked the door all the way open and they slowly went inside.

As they entered the hallway leading into the living room, Khalil saw that his apartment had been ransacked too. His furniture was overturned and some of his furniture had been ripped or knifed. As they walked deeper into the apartment they were met with a huge mess of things. Drawers been pulled out, tables overturned, his bedroom was in total shambles, covers pulled off the bed, TV pulled off the wall. He went into the bathroom where he still had a few thousand dollars put away for quick access down in the cabinet. The cabinet door was undisturbed, and Khalil breathed a sigh of relief.

"You should call the police," Omar said.

"Yeah, don't worry. That's exactly what I'm about to do."

Khalil felt it was Hezekiah and George's doing, although George was locked away. He then began to suspect if Dee had been in on this. She said she had nothing to do with his father but Khalil didn't believe a word coming out of her mouth. He would confront her, but first he needed to call the police.

Chapter 8

"Laws catch flies but let hornets go free." Scottish

The police came, dusted for fingerprints, took Khalil's report, and assured him they would do everything they could to find out who these thugs were that had confronted him outside his apartment. Khalil was told to come to the police station and look through mugshots to see if he could identify the dudes.

Next, after the police left, Khalil went to the church office. Once he arrived at Holy Rock, Khalil called Eliana into his office.

"I need a cleaning service at my apartment ASAP," he told her.

"Sure, I'll get right on it." She proceeded to get up from the chair but Khalil motioned for her to remain seated.

"That's not all. Are you available to go shopping?"

"Shopping?" she questioned.

"Yeah, shopping. I need to buy new furniture, bedding, and oh, I need you to call the same real estate agent that's helping my mom find a crib. I need one for myself... pronto.".

"Uh...okay," Eliana said, looking at Khalil strangely.

What exactly was he up to? What had happened? When he walked into the church that morning, he rushed in with a look of anger on his face. He barely spoke, something that was quite unusual for his fine behind. She was used to him smiling, telling her good morning, and complimenting her. That was not the case today. He looked flustered and quite upset. Now he wanted her to call a real estate agent and go shopping? Yea, something was totally out of sync.

"I'm on it," she said.

"When will you be available to go shopping with me?" he asked, finally releasing a smile so hypnotic she could barely respond.

"I'm...uh, whenever you say," she finally replied, pushing the words from her lips.

"Okay, first I want to talk to that real estate guy, and then when Omar comes, send him straight to my office. Cancel any appointments I have, including today's trustees' meeting. On second thought, get my mother on the phone. I'll have her sit in on the meeting."

"She's already in the office," Eliana informed him. "I'll go let her know you want to see her."

"Okay, cool. What about Xavier? Is he here too?"

"Yes, he's here. He's in a meeting with the Finance team. It's ten o'clock now, and he said he would be done by ten thirty, no later than eleven. Do you need me to interrupt him?"

Khalil showed his hands. "No, that won't be necessary. Just handle those things I asked and we'll go from there."

"Will do. Anything else?"

"No, that's it for now. Thanks, Eliana."

"No problem, Pastor Khalil."

"Khalil behind closed doors. Remember?"

"Yes, I remember…Khalil," she answered and walked off, blushing.

Khalil picked up the phone and called Dee, accusing her of plotting the whole thing with Hezekiah. Detria cried and sobbed while denying she had anything to do with the attempt to hurt Khalil. She begged him to believe her. By the time he got off the phone with her, he believed her, but even if he didn't, he remembered a saying that it's best to keep your enemies close. He knew one of the first things she would do would be to call or go see his father. That was playing right into his hands.

Omar arrived and the two of them sat down to make plans about what their next move would be. Without telling him that he knew the possible reason for the guys wanting to bring him harm, Khalil did tell Omar he believed his father was behind it.

"Your own father?" Omar said, pacing the floor of Khalil's office.

"Yeah, he's still mad about me taking over his ministry. I guess he still feels like me, my mom, and my brother are out to destroy him. I always knew he could get violent, but I guess since he couldn't handle things personally, he sent his goons to do it. But it's all good. I'm going to play my hand and believe me, I can hurt him far worse than he can hurt me and I don't have to lay a finger on him," Khalil said while tapping a pencil on his desk.

"Good morning, son," Fancy said after knocking on Khalil's door and opening it without waiting on him to say come in.

"Good morning, Mother."

"Oh, hello, Omar. How are you," she said when she saw him standing inside her son's office.

"Good morning, First Lady," Omar said, still acknowledging her as such although technically she was no longer the first lady.

"Omar, I'll get with you later. Oh, see Eliana. I need you to get the locks changed on my crib," he said. "I'll let the leasing manager know what happened a little later today."

'Sure thing, Pastor Khalil. Good day, First Lady," Omar said, tipping his head, and walking out of the door.

"Locks changed? What's going on, Khalil?"

Khalil told her what had happened minus the reason he believed he was targeted.

"Oh, my! Are you all right?" she asked, looking frantic and sounding upset.

Xavier appeared next, and again Khalil explained what had happened or almost happened to him.

"I don't know how far they would have gone," said Khalil. "All I know is my father, *our* father," he said, looking at his brother, "has gone too far."

"Yeah, way too far," Fancy said. "Something has to be done."

"Has the real estate agent found you a crib yet, Ma?" Khalil asked.

"Yes, I should be able to move into my own house in the next couple of weeks. It's in Lion's Gate in the Whitehaven subdivision."

"Yeah, I know where that is. But Whitehaven? You sure you want to live in Whitehaven?"

"Of course. I looked at several houses in Whitehaven when I first started this house search with Stiles. Whitehaven is a wonderful area of the city. Lion's Gate is still lovely, well-guarded, and quite safe—not to mention I'm tired of looking. I found a three bedroom, two bath home. Plenty of space for me and it was recently updated. I love it."

"That's good to hear, Ma," Khalil said and Xavier agreed.

"And you, bruh," Khalil said, turning his attention to Xavier.

"I was approved for my apartment and I'm moving next week."

"Sweetheart, you'll need to get furniture and dishes and utensils, towels, everything. We have to go shopping. Would you like to go when we leave here today?" Fancy asked, sounding excited and seemingly forgetting what Khalil had just shared with her and Xavier.

"Uh, Ma. I got this. I don't want to hurt your feelings, but me and a couple friends are going shopping. I've already been looking too. But I promise, if I need you, I'll let you know." He leaned over in his chair and kissed his mom on the cheek as she sat in the chair next to him. He hoped it would soothe her some.

"Look, I just wanted to fill you guys in on what happened. I got some things to take care of and we'll talk later. Ma, I'm going to use the same agent to find me something as soon as possible, even if I have to rent it until I find something permanent."

"Yeah, you cannot live in that apartment any longer. You should have no problem getting out of your lease," Fancy said.

"I know. Well, we'll talk later."

Khalil stood and taking queue from him, Fancy and Xavier rose and walked toward the door.

Khalil opened the door and Fancy walked out first.

"You sure you straight, bruh?" Xavier stopped and asked.

"Yea, I'm straight."

They gave each other dap and Xavier walked up the hallway with his mother while Khalil watched in the doorway of his office until they rounded the corner and disappeared.

Chapter 9

"Fate leads the willing and drags along the unwilling." Seneca

Detria had Priscilla to drive her to Hezekiah's place. She was livid that he had put her in the middle of his and his family's drama. The last thing she wanted was to alienate Khalil. She was getting back on track with him and now this.

Priscilla pulled up in front of the assisted living facility. Detria dashed out of the car almost as soon as the car stopped.

Rushing inside, she went to his apartment only to be met by a cleaning lady. She almost pushed the startled woman down as she stormed inside. "Hezekiah," she called. "Hezekiah," she called again.

"He no longer lives here," the perturbed woman said, eyeing Detria in displeasure.

"What? When did he move? Where did he go?" she asked, walking up to the woman like she was demanding her to answer.

"I don't know. Now if you'll excuse me, I have to get this place cleaned for the next tenant."

This time the woman walked past Detria, slightly brushing against her shoulder, and did not stop to look back.

Detria stormed out of the compact apartment and ran back to the car. She called Hezekiah on his phone.

"Hello there, my love."

"Where are you?" she asked. "I just left your place and they said you moved. Is there something you forgot to tell me?"

"Actually, no I didn't forget to tell you. I *chose* not to tell you. When I want you to know where I am, then I'll tell you where I am. Until such time, all I need you to do is what I tell you to do."

"You are so cruel and mean. How could you even fathom sending those men to beat up or worse try to kill your own flesh and blood?"

Priscilla listened as she drove. She couldn't believe what she was hearing. Then again, she heard so much private and sensitive information working for Detria Graham, none of which she repeated. She was loyal to Detria although she hardly ever agreed with the way the woman chose to live her life. She could be a good person if only she would learn how to love herself, but Priscilla could never convince her of that and had long since stopped trying.

"You're over exaggerating," Hezekiah rebuffed. "They were not going to kill him—just rough him up a little and get me my money. How saddened I am to hear that you would actually think I want to see my own son dead. Oh ye of little faith, my love."

"Well, just so you know, your plan didn't work. Khalil escaped from them but he thinks I had something to do with it."

"That's on you. I am not interested in you and my son. I don't give a care whether he takes every penny you have. I say, more power to him for his game. He got it from his poppa." Hezekiah laughed loudly into the phone.

"You low down, son of..."

"Hold up, watch your mouth," he warned, his tone suddenly turning serious. "You keep an eye on him and I want you to tell me every move that little prick makes that has to do with me. You understand?"

Detria remained quiet, listening to Hezekiah's stern instructions.

"Do you hear me?" he repeated.

"Yeah, whatever, Hezekiah. Goodbye."

"Goodbye, my love. I'll be in touch." Hezekiah smiled as he ended the call.

Hezekiah relaxed in his new home located thirty miles from Memphis and about twenty minutes from Isabella's spot in Arlington in a town called Piperton. With a caregiver who came three times a week for three hours a day and his young sidepiece, Isabella, he felt revitalized. His health was steadily on the incline and each day he felt better and stronger. He had the ability to transfer himself from the chair to his bed, or couch, and even into a car. Both arms were increasing in strength, except one was still a little weaker than the other. His speech was also improving. He had a deep slur, but he could be understood. He rarely used his oral device anymore to speak for him.

Hezekiah saw a speech therapist he found in Arlington three days a week, and an occupational therapist came twice a week. He had been approved for Medicaid and Medicare and received a monthly disability check from

Social Security, so he was straight. He rarely had to use the money he had put away and he made sure he stayed up on the latest ways to keep his money from being detected by Social Security and Medicaid. He had a bank account that his monthly disability check was deposited into, which was all he had going into that account. It wasn't the government or anybody else's business about what other money he had, and he had a substantial amount.

His son had escaped the two guys he had George to hire, but if Khalil thought he'd seen the last of him, he was sadly mistaken. He was going to get his money that the boy stole one way or the other. He might be able to run but Hezekiah said to himself *you sho can't hide.*

Isabella spent mostly Thursday through Sunday at Hezekiah's place rather than going back and forth to her home in Arlington. George had his friend, Benny, to pick her up and help out with Hezekiah in his absence. Being behind bars stopped very little of what George was able to get done on the outside. As long as Hezekiah continued to pay him by sending the money through his wife, and kept money on his books, he was straight.

There was a time Isabella was fascinated by Hezekiah because he was responsible for getting her off the streets, but when things took a sexual turn she learned quickly that he could be selfish, a demanding man, no better or different than the nameless other tricks she'd encountered since living on the streets. Yet, she felt a false sense of safety for her and her kid. Despite the tension, her life was better than the way it had been in the past. She wasn't on the streets, thanks to Hezekiah. He provided for her little boy—for her the good outweighed the bad.

Isabella, at the age of ten had completed fifth grade.

It was summertime when she escaped from her sexually abusive stepfather, and her verbally and physically abusive mother. She was a kid to her parents but on the streets she grew up fast. She had no trade, skills, and was functionally illiterate. She was quickly shown the major means of survival on the streets.

She had been attending Holy Rock for some time because Hezekiah had demanded she and the baby come. When he was Senior Pastor, he would have someone to pick her up and bring her to church almost every Sunday where she sat a few rows behind his wife. That all stopped when he had the stroke, and she hadn't been since then. She was glad. Attending that church made her feel like a phony and unworthy. She didn't ever see how God could love or forgive her for all the wrong turns she'd taken so she didn't want to hear anything about God.

"Isabella, I have a taste for some spaghetti and meatballs. Fix some coleslaw and green beans with that. Oh, and I want something sweet beside you, that is, for dessert," he ordered and laughed as he hung up the phone.

Isabella heard the threats he made to Detria. She knew very little of Detria, but just enough to know that whoever she was, she was also under Hezekiah's thumb.

Her toddler began crying. Isabella rushed to the back bedroom where the little boy had been sleeping.

"I don't want to hear that crying. Not again," Hezekiah said as Isabella raced to the back bedroom.

"He's just waking up from his nap," Isabella explained.

"Just keep him quiet. He cries all the time. It has to be something you're not doing right. A kid his age shouldn't be whining all the time. You have no parenting skills. Maybe you need to go back to what you know—laying on your back and living on the streets," he said loudly as he continued his attack although Isabella had disappeared into the bedroom.

Isabella wiped tears from her eyes as she listened to the mean words Hezekiah spewed. She picked up her crying little boy and hugged him close against her bosom. "Shhh, Momma's here," she said. "Momma's here."

"Come on out of there!" Hezekiah ordered. "Big Daddy's starving," he said.

Isabella returned to the living room where Hezekiah was seated in front of the mounted big screen television, watching a movie.

"Come here," he said to Isabella as she re-entered the room. She walked over to where he sat in his chair. "How about a kiss?" he said, sounding tender and quite nice.

That was one thing about Hezekiah, she never knew what bag he would come out of. Sometimes he was good as gold, treated her like she was the next best thing since sliced bread, and then other times he treated her like street garbage.

Isabella leaned in and reluctantly kissed him. He took hold of her and pulled her down on top of him while the little boy sat down in the floor and began watching the movie playing on the big screen.

His kiss was passionate, long, and deep. His hands glided over her body, taking in every curve, and becoming filled with desire. He couldn't perform intimately like he once did but it didn't stop him from doing whatever it took, or insisting that Isabella do whatever to satisfy his desires.

She gently eased out of his grasp. "Do you want me to make you something to eat or not?" she asked mildly. "And you see Tavius is in here," she said again, with a slight smile and looking at her little boy while Hezekiah's hands continued to roam over familiar places.

"I'm hungry for food...and for you," he said, looking into her eyes. He allowed her to get up from off his lap. "We'll finish later. Make sure you get that boy to bed early. I don't want to be disturbed tonight. I want you all to myself."

Chapter 10

"An ounce of blood is worth more than a pound of friendship." Spanish Proverb

Stiles called Fancy to see if she had moved into her new home.

"Hey," she said. "I'll be moving soon. Right now, I've been shopping and getting things in order, which means making sure I get everything in order for the moving company. They'll be doing all the work."

"Good for you. I hope you enjoy your new place. You know, Fancy, things may seem as if they're deteriorating around you, but God's got you. Hezekiah may have tried to ruin you, put you in a bad way, but look at how you're being blessed. You have a new home, and you don't have to be concerned with whether or not he's going to do something to try to pull the rug from underneath you again. You know what I mean?"

"Yeah, you're right. I thank God I was able to get this house. It's beautiful. It's so *me*," she said, and laughed.

"I can't wait to see it. Where is it anyway?"

"Whitehaven, inside Lion's Gate. Remember, it was the only one for sale there at the time."

"Yeah, I know, but when we saw it you didn't seem too impressed."

"It wasn't that I wasn't impressed. I guess it was because at the time I wasn't being forced out of my home, at least not to the point where I actually had a date to get out."

"I hear ya, but anyway, I think you made a good choice."

"Yes, because houses in that gated community don't come up for sale often, but that one was still on the market, and this time I decided not to pass it up. It was the two-story with the red brick, and long foyer that I loved. It had the swimming pool in the back yard and that beautiful lanai."

"Oh, okay, I remember."

"What about you? Have you given any more thought to Khalil's offer?"

"Yes, we've talked a few times about it, and I told him I wanted to make a visit to just talk face to face, talk to some of the staff ministers, and that sort of thing before I make my final decision."

"Sounds like you're definitely considering his offer."

"Ummm, I don't want to say. I'm not sure. I mean it has its perks, but then again, I still have some reservations, which is why I told him I wanted to spend some time talking to the other ministers on staff."

"I'm sure Khalil didn't object to that. I mean it's a reasonable request," Fancy responded.

"Oh, he was all for it, encouraged it even. All I have to do is come."

"How soon will it be before you come?"

"Soon, but I'll know more for certain after I talk to him. I suspect it'll be in the next couple weeks or so."

"Good," she said with excitement ringing in her voice. "Maybe you'll be here for my housewarming, nothing big. I invited some of the ministers, trustees, and deacons and their spouses or significant others. I would love if you were able to be here, too. It'll be my first time entertaining in my new home. I can't wait."

"I won't promise you, but I'll try. Let me talk to Khalil first and I'll get back to you. Okay?"

"Okay, great."

"So I take it you haven't heard anymore from my brother?"

"Not since I was served those papers, and as angry as I am at him, it's probably better if I don't. I don't know where he's living anyway."

"You don't?"

"Nope. I have no idea. I went to the last place I knew him to be and found out he was no longer there. Of course, they wouldn't tell me if they had a forwarding address or not. My lawyer told me not to worry; he'll get in contact with him. I'm not going to contest the divorce anyway. I just want out of the marriage. It might sound crazy, but I still love him."

"That's not strange. True love doesn't just up and disappear overnight. I still think Hezekiah's operating out of pride and haughtiness, which can cause a person to do things they wouldn't normally do or react in ways that are questionable. We have to keep praying for him that he'll come to his senses one day before it's too late."

"It might already be too late for us, but only God knows for sure."

"You never know, but just live your life, Fancy. Try not to stress or worry. I'm here for you. I've always told you that."

"Yes, you have and I thank you for your support. I really, really do. Just knowing I have you to talk to is a colossal weight off my shoulders."

"Bless you, Fancy. Well, look, I better call Khalil. You take care of yourself and we'll talk again soon, and remember, I'm always just a phone call or text away."

"I know. Thanks, Stiles. Buh-bye."

Ending the call, Stiles immediately called Holy Rock and asked for Pastor McCoy. Sista Mavis answered the call and led him into a conversation that went longer than he anticipated. In Sista Mavis fashion, she shared with him the latest gossip spreading around Holy Rock.

"I heard Pastor Hezekiah is in one of them god-forsaken nursing homes. That poor man has been abandoned by his family. Can you believe that, Pastor Stiles? And his wife, what kind of first lady would leave her husband to rot in one of them awful nursing homes? I tell you, it's a cryin' shame. Lord knows I wish you would come back."

Stiles couldn't get a word in edgewise as Sista Mavis kept babbling. "I'm sorry to hear about poor Pastor. Your daddy was a good preacher in his time," she said.

"What about my father?" Stiles asked, his listening ears suddenly interested in what Sista Mavis had to say about Pastor.

Sista Mavis grew quiet on the other end of the phone, but not for long. "All I can say is I'm praying for his wife. That lady is a strong woman. Having to take care of somebody that has Alzheimer's or dementia, whichever it is, has to be hard. I know my cousin has Alzheimer's. He wanders off, and he doesn't even know his wife and kids anymore. Lord, have mercy. I know you're a busy man, but I'ma tell you what God loves, Pastor Stiles…and that's the truth. You need to come to Memphis more often so you can help that poor woman, Josie, care for your father. She's not a spring chicken you know. And like my cousin, they ended

My Brother, Father...And Me 57

up having to put him away in one of those Alzheimer's facilities. It was for his own good."

"Thank you for the advice, Sista Mavis, but my father doesn't have dementia or Alzheimer's. He may forget some things but hey, we all forget from time to time. But, listen, you take care of yourself. It was good listen...I mean it was good talking to you. Now will you put me through to Pastor Khalil? he insisted, hoping he didn't sound too frustrated, but he was.

Stiles didn't care to entertain much of what Sista Mavis said, but the part about his father having dementia and Alzheimer's' struck a nerve. He couldn't deny that a time or two, maybe more, Pastor seemed more forgetful of things, but the man was in his seventies. Who wouldn't forget a thing or two at that age. Plus, Pastor had been devastated when he was basically excommunicated from the church he loved. That threw him for a big loop. Though he attended Holy Rock from time to time, Pastor and Josie never returned full time to the church after that. It was sad, and Pastor still had a hard time accepting it. If he did return to Holy Rock, he would have to make sure that Pastor and Josie felt comfortable enough to return to the church too.

Hearing what Sista Mavis said about his father, Stiles made a mental note to call Pastor after he spoke to Khalil.

"Hello, Unc, how's it going?" Khalil asked when he answered Stiles' call.

Stiles smiled to himself. Hearing Khalil call him Unc made him feel a little proud although Khalil's words sounded more like sarcasm rather than a genuine salutation. But Stiles would accept it for what it was.

"Hello, Khalil," he said in return. "How are things going?"

"Blessed. Like the older people say. Blessed and highly favored. I hope you're calling to tell me you've decided to accept the job offer."

"Not exactly," responded Stiles. "I'm still praying on it. Do you have a deadline?"

"No, not really, but the sooner I know where you're headed, the better. What's holding you up? You don't want to leave that chick you smashing in Houston?"

"I beg your pardon?"

"Don't try to sound all innocent, man. I know you got needs. Shoot, we all do. Pastors or not. You can be real with me." Khalil laughed.

"Naw, it's not like that. Me and her are strictly friends."

"Yeah, friends with some real good benefits." Khalil chuckled harder. "But that's not my concern. I just want you here, man. It's a lot going on. I could use your help."

"I take it your father—my brother—is still wreaking havoc even in his absence."

"Nothing I can't handle. So what's the reason for your call since you aren't calling to tell me you're coming back to Holy Rock?"

"I wanted to tell you to give me a few more days, maybe a week or so, and I'll have my answer. I also wanted to check on your mother. I spoke to her and she told me she was about to move. Is she straight? She sounded down, a little depressed. I know she's having it rough."

"Yeah, trying to deal with my father's antics has been hard on her, but I'm on it. Me and Xavier are making sure we keep an eye on her, take care of her, you know. Thanks for being concerned, but you handle your situation in Houston and let me and Xavier handle our mom."

Stiles detected some hostility in Khalil's voice. It

was somewhat understandable that he was protective of his mother but Khalil sounded like he thought Stiles had deeper interests in Fancy other than her being his sister-in-law. He thought about the kiss. It had definitely taken him by surprise. It was unexpected, the last thing he would have thought Fancy would have done, but he understood that a beautiful, sexy woman like Fancy had needs. If she wasn't his brother's wife, in another day and time, he would have made a play at her, would have taken the kiss she gave him a step farther, but he wasn't about to do that. He'd done it once when it came to Rena and his deceased sister, Frankie. Maybe he didn't know until later in his relationship with Rena that she had messed off with his sister for years, but when he did find out, it was heartbreaking. He refused to get himself tangled in a web like that ever again.

To this day, Rena still refused to talk to him, and that hurt Stiles every time he thought about her. The Jubilee Tragedy changed the lives of so many innocent people. He couldn't blame Rena for never wanting to see or hear from him again. She had told him every time she dealt with his family, she was put in the middle of mess and mayhem. His family, but especially him, had given her nothing but heartache.

As much as Stiles hated to think about it, he had to admit Rena was right. He thought she was his forever love, the one woman he would spend eternity with, but he managed to blow that to smitherings because he couldn't overlook her past with his sister. It was before he was even in the picture that she and Frankie messed off, but he treated her like she was trash, wouldn't forgive her past when his past was no better.

At one time he was nothing more than a playa, going

around bedding girls in college, leaving a trail of broken hearts yet he couldn't forgive Rena for her mistakes and foolish choices. He sometimes thought about how he had really made a mess of things between him and Rena, but it was too late now. No way could the hands of time be turned back. He had to move on with life, and he prayed that she was happy and content with her life. It was one of the main reasons he didn't want to invest in a real relationship again. He had been screwed over by the likes of Detria but he came to the conclusion that it was karma kicking him square in his behind because of his inability to forgive his ex-wife, Rena. Detria caused him much grief, heartache, and pain. Not so much because he was so deeply in love with her—he did love her at one time, but never the way he once loved Rena. He believed Detria sensed that so she never allowed herself to give her whole heart to him. She chose to give it to his friend, Skip, instead.

Stiles pushed the conversation with Khalil out of his mind for now and the thoughts about what could, would, or should have been with Rena and concentrated on Pastor. He dialed Pastor's phone and his father answered, sounding like a tired, old man. It was disheartening to hear.

"He…hello," Pastor said feebly into the phone.

"Hello, Pastor. How are you?" Stiles asked.

"To God be the glory," Pastor responded.

"Yes, that's right. To God be the glory," Stiles repeated.

"How are you feeling today?" Stiles asked again.

"Who am I talking to?"

Stiles dropped his head. Did Pastor just ask him who he was? Maybe Sista Mavis had been right after all. Could Pastor have dementia or Alzheimer's? Stiles shook his head in disbelief. No, Pastor was fine. He just didn't recognize his voice. Probably because of a poor phone connection.

"Uh, it's Stiles, Pastor."

"Stiles?"

"Yes, Stiles, your son."

"Stiles, oh yes, hello, son. How are you? What time are you going to be home?" Pastor asked.

Stiles held back tears. Was this Pastor? What was happening? He had just spoken to the man a few days prior to this call and he was fine, now this? Something was wrong, terribly wrong.

"Uh, remember, I'm in Houston, Pastor. I won't be there for a few weeks. Where's Josie?" Stiles asked.

"Josie? You mean, Audrey don't you, son? Your memory is failing you, isn't it?" Pastor laughed into the phone.

"Stiles," Josie said, suddenly on the phone.

"Josie, what's going on? Why is Pastor talking out of his head? Is he okay?"

"No, not really. We have an appointment at a neurology clinic day after tomorrow. He's been forgetting a lot lately, but the past few days he's like a different person. I was going to call you after I took him to the neurologist. I didn't want to worry you unnecessarily."

"I don't want you going through any of this alone, Josie. I've told you that before. I'll get a flight out and get there tomorrow sometime. This is the first time I've heard him talk like this. I mean he forgets from time to time. I was aware of that, but this is different. He didn't even recognize my voice, and he thinks you're Audrey?"

"Is Stiles all right, Josie?" Stiles heard Pastor ask in the background.

"See, he comes and goes. He's back to himself now."

"Woman, what are you talking about? What do you

mean I'm back to myself?" Stiles heard Pastor say to Josie. "Will you let me talk to my son, woman?" Pastor said, laughing lightly.

"Pastor?" Stiles said when Pastor returned to the phone.

"How are you, son?"

"I'm good. I was just telling Josie that I think I'm going to come home for a short visit. I'll catch a flight tomorrow."

"I always want to see you, son, but don't come here on account of me and Josie. We're fine. God's got us and you have a church to see to there in Houston. Me and Josie can take care of ourselves. The good Lord has been good to us."

"Yes, I know, Pastor, but I want to come. I'll stay a couple days and then I promise I'll fly back to Houston in time for Sunday service."

"You young folks are something else. Fly in, fly out. Like it's easy as one, two, three. Anyway, if that's what you want to do, me and Josie will be looking for you. Have you heard anything about your brother?"

"No, I haven't, but I have talked to Fancy and to Khalil. They're doing their best to cope with all the changes going on with Holy Rock, in their household and well, it's nothing to be concerned about. They're fine. All we can do is pray for Hezekiah that God will not only heal his body, but his mind, too."

"I touch and agree with you on that, son. It was good talking to you but I gotta hang up. It's time for Judge Mathis. You know me and Josie can't miss it." Pastor laughed heartily.

"Yes, sir, I know. Tell Josie I'll see her tomorrow if God says the same. Until then, take care of yourself, Pastor."

"I will, good bye, son."

Stiles was happy to hear his father talking normal again,

but it didn't erase his concern about Pastor's mental state. As soon as the called ended, he began searching for a nonstop flight out of Houston leaving first thing tomorrow.

Chapter 11

"Whoever controls the money controls you." Sharon Tucker

Khalil met with his mother, brother, and the trustees to discuss the embezzlement charges he recently raised against his father. Hezekiah wanted to play dirty so Khalil was about to show him who was the real boss.

He yielded the floor to his brother, the financial wizard. "After conducting a full financial review, it has been determined that over half a million dollars was embezzled by former Pastor Hezekiah McCoy. In addition, we have reviewed Holy Rock's financial accountability practices that protect the church and the reputations of any others involved with the church's finances."

Khalil then spoke up. "We considered one of two options and decided on the latter. The first option was to consider whether to involve local government authorities. If the amount stolen had been a small amount we more than likely would have decided to keep this matter private, asked for full repentance and restitution. This was not the case. The second choice is to entirely turn the matter over to the authorities and "wash our hands" of this terrible situation after being betrayed by my father, former Senior Pastor of this great church. After weighting both options, it is understandable that there comes a time, such as this, we thought it wise and in the best interest of Holy Rock to involve law enforcement, which we have done."

Many of the trustees present could be seen nodding in agreement. "Though it could have been done prematurely, a crime was still committed. I communicated this to the congregation of Holy Rock."

Xavier used his excellent mathematical skills to fix the financial records to show his father had embezzled hundreds of thousands of dollars, which would put Hezekiah behind bars far longer than the six years he once served!

Yeah, you messing with the wrong ones now, Daddy-o Khalil thought. All he had to do was find out where his father had moved. He had no real worries about that because he was assured by law enforcement and the FBI they would have no problem finding him. A search of Hezekiah's medical records would reveal that. Yep, it was only a matter of time and Hezekiah McCoy's walls would come tumbling down.

Khalil still couldn't believe his father would stoop to the low level that he had by sending those guys to do God knows what to him. Since that night, he made sure to look over his shoulder. He was about to move into his new spot this weekend. Holy Rock was footing the bill. Unlike his father, he wanted the church to pay the mortgage, taxes, and other expenses for his home. The trustees agreed without question. He had them in the palms of his hands. There was not much that they wouldn't agree to when it came to Khalil McCoy. He was just that smooth.

His next big purchase would happen later today after the meeting. He and Omar were headed to Brentwood, Tennessee to check out an $80,000 Tesla Roadster in his favorite color no doubt— red. He loved his Lexus coupe but in light of the vandalism that had been done to his 'baby' and the fact that the thugs knew the car, Khalil put it up for sale and got a buyer in a matter of days.

Xavier and Ian went shopping for furniture to put into his new crib. He was approved for his apartment the week after his mother purchased her new home. Each of them, including Khalil, were making money moves and Xavier felt good. He may have missed out on attending college, but he was quickly becoming accustomed to the benefits and perks of being part of Holy Rock. The more the church prospered, the more his pockets prospered…and the church was on the rise.

It was becoming a big draw, the church for young highly successful professionals and techies who didn't mind filling the collection plates Sunday after Sunday.

The television ministry would be taking off in another couple weeks and that was expected to bring in even more money. Televangelism was a billion dollar industry. Many pastors and churches became mega rich because of the reach these television preachers were able to garner. Khalil planned to be no different. He already had commercials he showed on two partner television stations announcing Holy Rock Ministries would be coming to those particular stations. He formed a partnership that was already starting to bring in substantial sums of money through social media, livestreaming church services, and mass mail outs. He and

Xavier, along with Fancy, of course, were turning Holy Rock into a church to be reckoned with.

Khalil arranged, along with Xavier, a partnership called WOW which stood for World of Worshippers. WOW were partners who sowed into the ministry of Holy Rock. They would receive a variety of gifts depending on the amount of their giving. His selling points to those who became WOW Partners was their donations and commitment to being WOW Partners would ensure Holy Rock was able to spread the Gospel of Jesus Christ globally, help those in need, support weekly television broadcasts, live worship events, and missions.

After each live and replayed television broadcast, much like he already started doing on Holy Rock's social media accounts, he offered tapes of his sermons and life changing messages, in exchange for any amount the person could give or at no charge. Most people, however, who ordered the tapes paid from one dollar to twenty-five dollars for each DVD which had grown into thousands being mailed. That too would only increase, Khalil guessed, when he went live on Sunday morning and did replays on Sunday evenings and live again on Wednesday nights.

The young preacher used the same hustle mentality he once used on the murderous and dangerous streets of Chicago and put it into making Holy Rock, but namely himself, a household name while his bank account grew exponentially.

"What about this?" Ian asked Xavier as they stopped and stood in front of a tan wraparound sofa Ian pointed out in the furniture store.

"Umm, I like it, but I don't know if my living space will hold such a huge sofa. I think I need something smaller."

"Yeah, I wasn't thinking about that. Your apartment is quite larger than mine so I thought it might work, but you're probably right, it wouldn't leave much room to get around. But I do love it," Ian told him.

They continued to walk around the furniture store. "What about this one? And that chair that goes with it? I think it'll be perfect," Xavier said as he pointed to an atomic red, three-seated, fabric sofa with high arm and headrests.

"Oooh, I love it. I see you have a wild side to you," Ian teased. "I never thought you'd like bright colors"

"There's a lot you've yet to learn about me," Xavier remarked, "stick around and you might find out."

"I can't wait," Ian replied. "So you're thinking about this one?" he asked, referring to the sofa again.

"Yes. I think it and the chair will be perfect. All we need to find now is a rug, a couple of end tables, and a coffee table."

"Let's do it then," Ian said.

Three plus hours later, Xavier had finished choosing the furniture, including a queen-sized bedroom set, a two seater dining room table, the sofa and chair and numerous other accessories. He made arrangements for the items to be delivered. Ian also helped him choose linen, towels, dishes, and anything else the two of them thought Xavier would need.

When he was done, he was exhausted, but happy that he was taking the step he was taking. He was a man, a man that would be living on his own, making his own money, and making his own decisions about his life. No more listening to the opinions of others; he was taking charge of his own life. With a friend like Ian, he felt empowered. Ian had that type of effect on him.

He was glad that Eliana introduced the two of them. Two more nights, and he would be picking up the keys to his own apartment. Settling down for the night, he fell asleep quickly at Ian's apartment.

Chapter 12

"Sometimes the heart sees what is invisible to the eye."
H. Brown, Jr.

"So you down with helping me out or nah?" Khalil flashed a *how-can-you-say-no* smile Eliana's way.

"I'm telling you, I'm not the decorator type. I like simple, down-to-earth kinda stuff."

"Sooo, what you're saying is I'm materialistic, flashy, and uhh, a poser, huh?" He laughed again.

"Uh, I wouldn't exactly say you like simple. Didn't you tell me a few days ago that you were going to that Tesla dealership up in Brentwood? I mean those cars are not exactly simple, you know. And the car you had, that red Lexus Coupe wasn't exactly comparable to my beat up Honda Accord," Eliana said, with a bright smile of her own that made Khalil want to get next to her even more.

"Okay, you got me there. But hey, I can't help that I like the finer things life offers."

"And you're saying I don't?" Eliana looked at Khalil, folded her arms inside each other, and gave him a cute little smirk.

Khalil laughed. "I wasn't saying that. Come on, let's go inside this store and pick out some things for my new crib."

He invited her to come along with him and give him advice on picking out some pieces for his house as an excuse to spend time with her outside of Holy Rock, feel her out, and get to know her a little bit more. So far since she became his full time administrative assistant, she kept their relationship on a strictly professional basis. He basically did the same thing. It wasn't that he didn't want to get to know her but so much was going on in his personal life because of the actions of his father. His mom and brother having to up and move at a moment's notice and his dad filing for divorce weighed heavily on Khalil's mind and heart. He felt bad for his mom; she loved Hezekiah and Khalil could see the strong front she was trying to put up. Now that she was moving into her own space, he hoped she would start to concentrate on rebuilding a life without Hezekiah McCoy, get some friends, and enjoy the blessings of God. He didn't know if that would happen. This would be the first time since meeting and marrying Hezekiah that she would be living alone. With Xavier having his own spot, it was either going to be a good thing for their mother or she was going to spiral downward into a depression. He prayed that it wasn't the latter.

"Your closing is coming up soon isn't it?" Eliana said, as Khalil opened the door to the store.

"Yeah, in less than a week."

"Seems like the whole family is making moves into new homes. God is really blessing," Eliana said.

"Yeah, He is. Xavier just secured his own spot in the same complex where you live. My mother found a new home, and I'm happy for her. And me, God has blessed me to buy my first home, too. His favor is in the air. It's spreading all over us, and I couldn't be happier."

Khalil and Eliana walked through the large space filled with all types of furniture.

"You like this?" Eliana asked, pointing to a posh chair that turned out to be a recliner.

"Yeah, I do. I can see myself laid back in this chair in my man cave, watching television, the playoffs, or Netflix. Yeah, this is nice. Looks like I brought the right person along," he said jokingly.

Eliana smiled, hoping her secret affection for Khalil wasn't too obvious. When he asked her if she would accompany him to look for furniture and appliances, she couldn't have been more excited, but she tried to play it off and act nonchalant about his invitation. She walked next to him, imagining things were far different than they were. Her brother seemed to be hitting it off with Xavier. What was the hold up with her and Khalil? She chalked it up to being that her and Khalil's relationship was different because she was Khalil's employee and in his position, it would be frowned upon, she was sure, by many at Holy Rock. Like Sista Mavis. Sista Mavis would have a raging fit if she thought Eliana and Khalil had something going on. It wasn't that she cared what others thought of her, but then again, she wanted to maintain a stellar reputation for being a young, faithful, and committed employee and woman of God. She couldn't do that if she started messing around with the senior pastor. There were enough girls who pranced themselves in front of Khalil already. She didn't want to be one of those.

"I like this, too," Khalil said pointing to a classy, high end, sofa.

They continued walking, looking at furniture when the both of them saw Xavier and Ian walking up.

"Hey, what are you two doing?" Eliana asked as they approached.

"I could be asking you the same thing, sis," Ian said, embracing his sister and then stepping back and extending his hand toward Khalil's. "Hello, Pastor Khalil."

Khalil didn't extend his hand. He pretended that he didn't notice Ian's gesture.

"What's up, bruh?" Xavier said. "Hi, Eliana." He hugged her in the same manner as Ian.

"You doing some shopping, too, huh?" Khalil said without saying a word to Ian. He couldn't shake it. He hated that his li'l bro was gay. It rubbed him the wrong way and seeing him and Ian together made him even more irritable. It wasn't right. It didn't feel right; look right; and in God's eyesight it wasn't right. It was totally unnatural and he couldn't shake that feeling. He didn't want to come off as being judgmental, but it was how he felt and so there it was.

"Yeah, I found some things. What about you?" He looked at his brother and then over at Eliana. "I see you brought some help along, too." He smiled again at Eliana and she did the same in return.

"Yeah, I asked her to come help a brother out. I didn't want to bother Mom. I know she has a lot going on with trying to get things set up for her own space. You talk to her today?"

"Yeah, for a few minutes this morning," Xavier responded.

"Cool. Well, look, I'll talk to you later. I want to find a few pieces and then get out of here. I don't want to spend my whole Friday in a furniture store. Know what I mean?"

"Yeah, I feel ya." Xavier looked over at Ian, and fist

bumped him on the side of his shoulder. "You ready?"

Ian rolled his eyes at Khalil. He felt the coldness Xavier's brother gave him. He could tell Khalil wasn't feeling the friendship he and Xavier had, but Ian didn't care. He had long since stopped worrying or being concerned about what others thought about his lifestyle.

"Yes, I'm ready. Suddenly, I'm cold. I feel a chill up in here," he said.

Khalil picked up on the snide remark. He started to say something to him but decided against it. If he stood a chance, any chance, of getting Eliana to warm up to him and give him a chance, then he needed to maintain control of his ill feelings toward her brother.

Eliana swiftly glanced at Khalil. She noticed the looks her brother gave Khalil and the biting look he gave Ian in return. She didn't like that the two men were already at odds without either of them taking time to know each other. Eliana loved her brother deeply. It didn't matter to her one way or the other what his life choice was, as long as he was happy. She hoped Khalil could feel the same way about his brother. Xavier seemed like a really nice guy and she was genuinely praying that he and Ian would become good friends if nothing more. It seemed like that prayer was being answered as she said goodbye to the two guys and watched them walk away laughing and talking.

"They seem like they really like each other," Eliana said when her brother and Xavier walked out of earshot.

"Whatever floats their boats," Khalil said.

"I'm sorry you feel that way."

"Feel what way?" Khalil said. "To each his own. I just don't know how a dude—or a female—can get off on laying up next to someone of the same sex. It doesn't make sense.

Anyway, if they good with it, then I'm good with it. It's just that I'd prefer laying up against a soft, sweet smelling, beautiful woman," he flirted.

Eliana blushed but didn't say anything in response.

Khalil noticed her quietness but he also noticed her turn a shade darker when he said what he said. She was either embarrassed or feeling him. He preferred to think that she was feeling him. He would keep playing his cards slow and easy before he went for the kill and swooped her off her feet.

Chapter 13

"What you are will show in what you do." Thomas Edison

Hezekiah and Detria exchanged light conversation while Benny drove them to the Federal Correctional Institute in Millington, Tennessee where George was serving his time. It was about a thirty-minute or so drive outside of Memphis. Detria didn't want to go but like he always did, Hezekiah had insisted.

Why did she continue to allow him to manipulate her like she was his woman when clearly she wasn't. She was glad the stroke rendered him unable to perform, well unable to perform fully. The less he made advances toward her, the more relaxed she could be in that sense. However, he still made her uncomfortable because he knew about her love for white powder and he fed into that constantly. It was George's dealer, the same guy who was driving them to Millington, that was her dealer...and Hezekiah's too, except Hezekiah wasn't gung-ho over indulging as much as she was. He preferred to lace his weed with the powder whereas she loved to snort it as much and as often as she could. It was one of the things she kept from Khalil. If he found out she was a cokehead, she believed her mission to become his wife would go down the drain. She couldn't have that.

The other thing Hezekiah and George held over her head was her involvement in stealing from the church. She started helping Hezekiah soon after he took on the role of senior pastor at Holy Rock. She told him about the bank accounts the church had, who was privy to them, and how he could gain total access to the millions of dollars that filtered through the church. The three of them laundered their dealer's money through Holy Rock, or they used to until Hezekiah's stroke and Khalil assumed the role as pastor. It was enough to put her behind bars if she didn't do what Hezekiah and George told her.

"When are you going to tell me where you moved, Hezekiah?"

"When I get good and ready. Right now, I don't see the need for you to know where I lay my head just as long as I know where you lay yours. Speaking of a place to lay my head, I thought I'd lay over at your place this weekend."

Detria looked at him suddenly. Her eyes surely revealed her surprise and so did her mouth as it gaped open.

"Be careful, you don't want a bug to fly into your mouth," he said, laughing as he looked back at her from his front seat view. "You got a problem with that?"

"I do have a life, you know."

"If you're talking about a life with my son, then you're fooling yourself, sweetie. Anyway, I don't care what life you have, this weekend your life is going to be centered around me, so tell Miss Prissy Priscilla what's up. Get her to make me her classic, soulful meal of turnip greens, cornbread, fried chicken and sweet potatoes. That woman knows she can burn," he said, licking his lips. "Oh, and for my sweet tooth, get her to make one of those scrumpdelicious butter pound cakes."

"Hezekiah, please. I told you, this weekend is not good," Detria insisted. She had plans to get Khalil in her bed and now Hezekiah wanted to throw a wrench into that.

"I guess you think I stutter," he said, looking at her and giving her the evil eye while the dealer driver looked through the rear-view mirror, smiled, and shook his head.

Don't she know yet not to cross Hezekiah McCoy, Benny thought.

"Hezekiah, no, I don't think that at all, but I already have plans. Why can't you come stay a couple days during the week? That'll be better. I promise I'll make it up to you if you just let me have this weekend for myself."

"And I just told you to make sure Priscilla makes my favorite meal. Whatever you got going on this weekend can wait. Benny," he said to the driver. "You got a little something that'll make her feel better? Something that'll calm her anxious behind down."

Benny reached for the small pouch inside his pocket, removed a vial, and passed it to the backseat where Detria was seated.

"Try this," Benny said. "Man, this is some powerful stuff. Just got it in last night. Uncut, too."

"Shoot, I want some of that myself," Hezekiah said, "but ladies first."

He didn't have to say it twice because Detria had quickly reached toward the front seat, took the pouch out of Benny's hand and opened it. She removed the vial, turned the top on it, and quickly used the tiny spoon that was built into the vial to snort as much of the powdery substance as she could. She leaned her head back against the soft back seat, closed her eyes, and allowed the drug to do its thang.

"Hold up, don't hog the stuff. Give it here," Hezekiah

said. Detria took another deep snort and then passed it up to Hezekiah.

"What you gone do with this?" Hezekiah asked. "You can't have this in the car when we get there."

"Yeah, I know. I thought you two would have been done with it before we got there."

Hezekiah laughed as he began feeling the drug's powerful effects. "You hear that Dee? Looks like we have our job cut out for us."

Detria, didn't open her eyes. Her head remained against the back seat. "Let's do it." She plugged one end of her earbuds into her phone and the buds into her ears. She turned on the music in her phone's playlist. She snorted more of the white powder when Hezekiah passed it back to her.

Before they arrived at the federal prison, Benny pulled over into the driveway of a wooden bungalow style house. "This is my partner's crib, the one I told you about," he said to Hezekiah.

"Yea, I know dude. George introduced me to him a few times."

"We can hang here for a minute. Give you two some time to get yourself together before we hit the prison. I have to drop off a package and I'll leave that pouch here, too, that is if y'all don't finish it all."

"It's a little much for me," Hezekiah admitted. "You know how I prefer mine. But sweetpea back there might feel differently."

Feeling good and high, Detria laughed. "A couple more hits and I'll be good," she said, then opened the door and climbed out of the back seat.

Benny popped the trunk, got out of the car, and retrieved

Hezekiah's wheelchair.

The three of them went inside the house and hung out until it was close to the prison camp's visiting hours. They were less than fifteen minutes away.

Detria went to the bathroom before they left, rinsed her face with cold water using her good hand, made sure her waterproof makeup was still flawless, and then came out and told the guys she was ready whenever they were.

"Game on. Time to go see how old George is turning up," Hezekiah said, chuckling.

Chapter 14

"Take the first step in faith. You don't have to see the whole staircase, just take the first step." M. L. King

Fancy surveyed her new surroundings. She'd just closed on the house earlier that week and now she was waiting on the movers to deliver her furniture. The furniture she removed from her old house, she decided not to keep. Initially, she was going to keep it for her new digs, then she decided she would offer it for sale on Craigslist, but after giving it more thought, she made the final decision to practically give it all away for pennies at Holy Rock's annual flea market. The flea market brought in hundreds of people looking for the best bargains. Though the furniture cost a pretty penny of Hezekiah's money, she pulled a Bernadine Harris move and sold most of the items for as little as fifty cents. Bernadine Harris was the character Angela Bassett played in the 1995 classic hit, "Waiting to Exhale." When the last piece was sold, she exhaled deeply, smiled in satisfaction, and strutted to her car. *Two can play this game*, she thought.

She walked through her empty new house and prayed in each room, anointing the frames of the rooms with blessed oil. Her heart was overcome with a mixture of sadness and joy. Sadness because moving into this house meant her life as she'd known it with Hezekiah had come to an end. It signified that things were about to take on a newness she was not sure if she was prepared for. She had lived her life with Hezekiah, the man of her dreams, her support, her stabilizer, her husband, lover, and even her minister and pastor. Now all of that was gone, no more, and she didn't know how she would handle it. Sure, Hezekiah had been gone physically for at least a year. It had been that long since his stroke, but in the beginning, she thought things would go back to normal and his recovery would be complete. He would take his reign in the pulpit of Holy Rock once again and their life as the First Couple would resume. None of that happened. Everything she planned, dreamed, and hoped was gone. She was left in this empty new house with a broken, hurting heart, and only God to rely on. That's where her joy came from—God. The joy was what she would rely on to see her through this transition, this new phase of her life. Joy in God was what would keep her on her feet, keep her standing, and keep her mind strong. Joy was something that no one, not even Hezekiah, or herself, could take away because it wasn't man who gave it to her— it was God. The doorbell rang as she anointed the doorframe of the last room.

She closed the top on the oil, put it inside her fashionable wide leg pant pocket, and hurried to the door.

"Hi, Ma," each one of her sons said when she opened the door.

"I thought you were the movers," she said to her sons as she opened the door wider, stepped aside, and allowed them to come inside the house.

"They haven't been here yet?" Xavier asked.

"No, but they should be here soon. They said between

noon and four. You know how that goes."

"Yeah, tell me about it. How are you doing, Ma?" Khalil continued to walk inside the house, looking around the empty space as he spoke.

"I'm good."

"You sure you're okay, Ma?" Xavier followed up.

"Yes, thank you for asking. I'm so glad the two of you came over."

"We told you we would," Khalil said.

"Yeah, I know, but I'm just saying... it's good to see the two of you. Sometimes it feels like I don't get the chance to spend time with you outside of Holy Rock."

"That's because that's where the three of us spend a majority of our time," Khalil said. "Mind if I go upstairs and take a look around?"

"No, of course not. You've seen everything, but help yourself. It'll all come together once the furniture is delivered.

"Mind if I say a blessing over it?" Khalil asked.

"That would be wonderful." She didn't mention she had already anointed the rooms. She welcomed the idea that her son even offered. He had grown so much in his ministry and his faith in God. She was overjoyed and overwhelmed at the same time.

"Do you two want to follow me? I'm going to say a prayer over each room, anoint it with this oil I bought." He pulled a vial of oil out of his pocket and held it up for Fancy and Xavier to see.

"Yes, we'll follow you. Where two or more are gathered, we know our God is in the midst," Fancy added, smiling broadly.

She took hold of Xavier's hand and the two of them

followed Khalil to each room. As he prayed, Fancy began
to cry softly. She thanked God inwardly for all he was doing
in the lives of her sons. Xavier and Khalil were proving to
be outstanding young men and she couldn't be happier.

When he was finished blessing the rooms upstairs, they
returned downstairs and Khalil repeated the same.

"Thank you, son," she said and hugged Khalil. "Thank
you, too, Xavier."

"You're welcome, Ma. Keep the faith, things are turning
around for the three of us. Good things are about to explode
in our lives. You wait and see."

"Yeah, Ma, Khalil is right. I believe things are looking
up for us. We all are starting new paths but we're still a
family. I know it's hard living without Dad, but you're
going to make it. You have me and Khalil. Don't you ever
forget that. We'll always be here for you."

Fancy released the tears this time. "You two are so
amazing." She walked into the kitchen. "Come on, I may
not have furniture yet, but I do have a refrigerator full of
food, and I brought some paper plates, plasticware, and
cups to have something to eat with. I can make you some
sandwiches while we wait on the movers."

"Sounds good," Xavier chimed in first.

"Yeah, your sandwiches are the best," Khalil said,
reminding Fancy of when they were little boys. Dem McCoy
boys, people in the neighborhood would call them when the
boys were growing up in Chicago. They were always into
something, keeping Fancy and Hezekiah on their toes.

Fancy opened the fridge and removed several items and
began making turkey and cheese sandwiches for her sons.

"Look in the cabinet to the right, Khalil and, get the
paper plates and cups. Look in the pantry over there,

Xavier." She pointed. "I think that's where I put the plastic forks and spoons."

"Yes, ma'am," they each replied.

When she was done, she walked over to the stocked pantry and removed two types of chips, corn chips and plain potato chips. She put them on the kitchen island next to the plate that held several sandwiches and then ordered her sons to sit at the island and help themselves.

"Aren't you going to eat?" Xavier asked.

"No, I'm good. I'll eat something later. I was thinking about going out this evening after the furniture arrives. A couple ladies from the Women's Ministry invited me to go with them to celebrate Sista Mavis' 60th birthday. Several women from the ministry will be there."

"Good for you," Khalil said. "I know Sista Mavis will get a kick out of having you there. She may not be able to hold water, but she's still a faithful member."

"Yes, she is. She may be the church gossip but she has a heart of gold. Really she does," affirmed Fancy.

"I like Sista Mavis," Xavier said, "as long as her lips aren't moving."

They laughed at Xavier's joke.

"Seriously, I hope you do go, Ma."

"I'm going. I need a break from all of this."

"Yeah, you do," Xavier agreed. The doorbell chimed. "I'll get it. It's probably the movers."

"I sure hope so," Fancy countered.

Khalil took a huge bite of his sandwich followed by a handful of potato chips, stuffing his mouth.

"Take your time, Khalil. The food isn't going anywhere." She laughed as she thought how Khalil always stuffed his mouth from the time he was a little boy.

"Good afternoon, come in," she and Khalil heard Xavier say.

Fancy and Khalil walked out of the kitchen and went into the foyer where they saw Xavier talking to one of the movers.

"We wanted to make sure someone was here. Give us a few minutes to start unloading, and we'll be inside."

"Sure, no problem," Xavier said.

"Oh, while my men are unloading, can me and Jim come inside so you can tell us where you want the furniture placed?"

"Yes, of course. My mom is right there," he said, looking back and pointing to Fancy. "She'll show you where everything goes."

The lead man looked at the guy standing next to him. "Come on, Jim." They walked inside, following Xavier.

Fancy took the lead and showed the two men where she wanted everything placed. It took several hours but finally everything was put together and in its perfect place. The house finally looked like a home.

"Ma, this place looks straight," said Xavier. "It looks like a house that would be in one of those home magazines."

"Yeah, you have real good taste, Ma. Xavier's right, this place looks like it should be showcased in a magazine or on DIY."

"I don't know about all of that, but I must admit everything came together nicely. The movers did a great job. Everything is just as I wanted. Praise God."

"They put everything up, too, including hanging your clothes in the closet, putting up all those hundred pairs of shoes you have, putting linen in the closets…"

"Yeah, they did it all. Wow, all you have to do is sit back

and relax."

"I hope you're going to have them do the same when you move," Fancy said, looking through each of the rooms.

"Yea, I am. I don't know if those same men will come, but I know it's the same company. Holy Rock, from what some of the older members told me, has been using this company for a minute now."

"Yes, they're the same company that moved your father and me into our house. They did an excellent job back then, too." She felt herself tearing up again as she thought about how happy she and Hezekiah were back then, but she forced herself not to cry. She wanted this day, though bittersweet, to be a good one.

"We're going to get out of here so you can get ready to go hang out with Sista Mavis and the other ladies."

"Let me pack the rest of those sandwiches. It's enough for both of you."

"You sure?" Xavier asked.

"Yes, I'm not going to eat them."

"Cool."

"Nothing but a word," Khalil said, and they retreated to the kitchen.

Chapter 15

"Oh, my friend, it's not what they take away from you that counts. It's what you do with what you have left."
Hubert Humphrey

Weeks passed. Xavier, Fancy, and Khalil had each moved into their new homes.

Xavier had a small housewarming, one that he invited his brother and mother to attend.

Eliana hoped she would see Khalil this evening and was a little disappointed when he told her he had a meeting with Stiles Graham, and wouldn't be able to attend. At his request, she brought Khalil's gift for his brother with her to the housewarming. She noticed Khalil was increasingly relying on her to take care of personal matters, and she welcomed it. It was a chance for the two of them to get to know each other more and spend more time together. He'd yet to ask her out, but she felt that it was only a matter of time before he did.

Stiles was scheduled to come to Memphis and the two of them, along with several of the trustees and Omar were going to meet over dinner. Eliana didn't know Stiles Graham, personally, but she knew that he used to be the senior pastor of Holy Rock and was the brother of Hezekiah

McCoy. She also knew about the Jubilee Tragedy because it made national news. She googled it before she started working at Holy Rock and learned all about the sad day and the victims of the tragic event.

She helped Xavier and Ian prepare the food. There were only about ten people who attended, but members of Holy Rock had been sending tons of gifts, gift cards, and money when they found out Xavier was getting his own spot. They did the same thing for Khalil, only on a far greater scale, and again the same for Fancy.

Fancy hoped to have a chance to see Stiles while he was in Memphis, but for now, her main focus was on supporting her baby boy. She showed up at Xavier's apartment with an armful of gifts.

Holy Rock loved the McCoy family even though Hezekiah McCoy was no longer part of the great church. *How soon people forget.*

Eliana arranged food on the six-foot table they borrowed from the church along with chairs for all the guests.

Fancy joined Eliana in the kitchen and offered her assistance. Anything to get closer to the McCoy family was welcomed by Eliana. The last thing she wanted was for First Lady McCoy to dislike her for any reason just in case she and Khalil became an item.

"My son likes you," Fancy said out of the blue as they arranged the last items of food and beverages on the decorated table.

Trying to keep from sounding surprised, Eliana responded, "I love working for Holy Rock. Pastor Khalil is easy to get along with, and he's such a thoughtful, kind, and considerate man."

Fancy watched as the young girl blushed. She could

easily sense that Eliana liked her son. She'd noticed it before tonight, but she hadn't addressed it. She was okay with the fact that Eliana liked Khalil. If only she could get Khalil to settle down and concentrate on finding a first lady, then all would be well. If that young lady was Eliana, Fancy thought it would be even better. Eliana was smart, bright, and since her short time at Holy Rock, the girl had learned more about the church or just as much about it as Sista Mavis and some of the other long time members. Fancy also liked the fact that Eliana wasn't a gossip. She could be relied on to keep confidential matters confidential. That was a huge plus.

"I'll put in a good word for you," she whispered and smiled at Eliana.

Eliana blushed again. "I...I don't know what to say." She didn't want to tell the first lady that she was right when she said she liked Khalil, but she was glad the woman saw through her and gave her approval.

"You don't have to say a thing, my dear. Let's just say it's written all over your face, and honestly, I think you would make a good wife for my son. There's only one thing I'd love you to do."

"What is that, First Lady?"

Fancy looked around. Xavier was being the perfect host and that boy, Eliana's brother, was right next to him. He barely gave Xavier room to breathe. The doorbell rang on and off almost constantly as Xavier...and Ian welcomed the invited guests into Xavier's apartment.

"I know there has to be a young lady as lovely as yourself that you can introduce to Xavier. I mean he's somewhat shy, and you know he won't listen to his mother. I'm too antiquated in my thoughts. At least that's what he thinks,"

Fancy said, trying to sound coy but at the same time giving a 'you know what I'm getting at' kind of look at Eliana.

Eliana began to feel uncomfortable. She was not slow by a long shot. She understood perfectly what Fancy McCoy was saying—she didn't want Xavier and Ian together. Eliana had heard Sista Mavis one time talking about Xavier and how word around Holy Rock was that he was gay. She sensed Khalil's apprehension about his brother's sexuality as well, and now she was hearing that same disdain from his mother. She didn't want to be in the middle of anyone's personal affairs unless it was her own, but she was not about to go against anything Fancy McCoy threw out there. If she expected to have a chance with Khalil, she would have to help Fancy carry out whatever scheme she had up her sleeve.

"You're a beautiful young lady. You're about to graduate with your master's degree. There has to be someone, one of your friends from college, church...someone that will be a perfect match for Xavier. He's quite a catch, too. Wouldn't you agree?"

"Yes...yes, ma'am."

"Thatta girl. I can't wait until you and Khalil are married and giving me some grandbabies." Fancy laughed and slightly elbowed Eliana.

Eliana returned the smile. She couldn't wait until that day either. *Game on.*

Chapter 16

"The winds of heaven change suddenly; so do human fortunes." Chinese saying

Stiles and Khalil finished their meeting with the trustees. Afterwards, they joined Omar for a game of pool at one of the local billiard rooms.

"I hope we answered all your questions and concerns, and that now you'll make the final decision to come back to Holy Rock. We can use a good, strong man of God like you on our team, Stiles," Khalil told him as he drove Stiles to Pastor and Josie's house.

"I'll have my decision for you in a couple more days for sure."

"That's straight," Khalil stated.

"How's your mom?"

"She's good. Settling into her new spot."

"I think that's a good thing. Staying busy should help to keep her mind off of my brother and their divorce."

Khalil didn't particularly like the fact that his mother shared her personal business with Stiles. It wasn't that he thought ill of Stiles, but he didn't fully trust him around his mother. It was too easy for people with broken hearts to be vulnerable. Men like Stiles could easily take advantage of

Fancy and that was one thing Khalil wasn't having. If Stiles returned to Holy Rock he would make sure that Stiles kept his distance from his mother.

"Thanks for dinner and the game of pool. I'll see you tomorrow," Stiles said.

"Yeah, I'm looking forward to tomorrow."

"Me too. I appreciate the invitation to share the word with the people of God."

"That's why I want a man of your statue to be the assistant pastor. You have a lot to offer and like me, you preach practical sermons that today's people can relate to. Tomorrow will be just a taste of what we talked about. You said you didn't want to commit to having to preach once a month, so instead when I go on sabbatical which I will start doing two weeks during the fall, two weeks during the summer, and one week in the winter, I'll look for you to run all three services. Of course, as we discussed, you still won't have to preach at every service during my absence but you will make sure one of the ministers is equipped and ready to deliver a powerful word. During my absence I would also like you to be available and in Memphis as much as possible."

"Yes, that was made clear. What I might consider doing is scheduling my sabbaticals from Full of Grace so it will coincide with your sabbaticals."

Yeah, that's a good idea. I hope you'll still be able to get a little R and R while you're here. I think with God's help you can do it."

They arrived at Pastor's house.

"How is the old man?" Khalil asked when he pulled up into Pastor's driveway.

"He's good. He misses being on staff at Holy Rock. He

misses the church overall."

"My pops is gone. Tell your father that he and his wife are welcome to attend Holy Rock anytime. I think I've seen him a few times since I took over the ministry.

"Yeah, you have. He comes more than he used to, but he and Josie still visit other churches."

"That's understandable. When a person is hurt, especially *by* the church, it can be difficult to return to that church and become an active member. Sometimes people stay away from the church as a whole, and from God."

"Yeah, they do. You know, you're a wise man for your young age, Khalil. If I haven't said it before, I want you to know you're doing a phenomenal job. Your membership has excelled and the times I've livestreamed church services, your messages are relevant, practical, and life changing."

Hearing Stiles tell him that he was proud of him and calling him wise was a big deal for Khalil. It made him feel that he was doing exceptionally well for a guy who had no ministerial experience, and not even one single theology class."

"Thanks, Stiles."

"It's the truth. You're achieving greatness by leaps and bounds. To be starting your own televangelism ministry is huge, man! That's something I've always dreamed of and here you are doing it. God is showering you with favor, Khalil."

"And think about it, as assistant pastor of Holy Rock, you'll be part of that too."

Stiles nodded, smiled, and then opened the passenger side of the car. "Oh, another thing. Man, this ride is unbelievable. This thing is *sweeeet!*"

"Yeah, it is," Khalil chuckled. "What can I say other

than God is good."

"All the time," Stiles said, stepping fully out of the car and closing the door behind him.

Khalil let down the window of the passenger side. "You need me to send someone to swoop you up in the morning?"

"Naw, man. I'm straight. Remember, I rented a car while I'm here. It's nothing like this baby here, but it'll get me from point A to point B," Stiles laughed again, waved his hand, and walked to the entrance leading to Pastor's side door.

"Okay, I'm out," Khalil said, and then exited the driveway.

"Stiles, is that you?" Josie said as she approached the side door.

"Yes, ma'am, it's me."

Josie opened the door dressed in a heavy purple robe, with rollers peeking out from underneath a black satin bonnet.

"How was the meeting?" she asked as she ushered him inside.

"It was, well it was much better than I anticipated. Things went so well that it gives me that much more to think about."

"Think about but mainly pray about," Josie mildly corrected.

"Yes, that's right—pray about. Where's Pastor?" he walked through the living room, following behind Josie with each step. "Sleep?"

"No, he's in the den watching an episode of 48 Hours. You hungry? I made a pot of vegetable stew and some buttered cornbread. There's an apple cobbler on the stove too."

96 Shelia E. Bell

"I should say I'm not hungry, but then again I always have room for some of your cooking."

"I'll fix you a plate. You go on in the den and talk to your father."

"No, I can fix my own plate, Josie. You go back and sit down or go back to doing whatever it was you were doing. I'm a big boy. I can do this."

"Nonsense. I'm the elder here. You do what I say," she said, heading for the kitchen.

"Josie?"

"What is it?"

"How is he really?" he said in a low, controlled tone.

"I'm worried. I know the neurologist says not to get all frantic about it, but I can't help it; I'm scared."

The day he arrived in Memphis was the day of Pastor's neurology appointment. Stiles accompanied Pastor and Josie. Several tests were administered. During the three-hour plus visit, Pastor became highly irritated and short tempered, which was uncharacteristic of him. He was known to be an even-tempered and patient man, but the day of his appointment showcased a totally different man. He demanded that Josie take him home. The more she tried to explain that there were more tests to be ran, the more upset he became until Stiles stepped in, talked to Pastor, and managed to get him to calm down.

At the end of the doctor's visit, the neurologist, a patient, understanding, and seemingly knowledgeable Indian physician, explained how the diagnosis would be determined. Pastor appeared irritated but remained quiet but with deep furrows lining his face.

"First, let me say this—there is not a single test that determines whether an individual has dementia. There are several forms of dementia with Alzheimer's being one of them. A diagnosis is made based on several factors. Those factors are the patient's medical history, a neurological and physical examination, which we carried out today. There are also laboratory tests we use such as what we also administered today."

"The blood tests and brain imaging?" Stiles added.

"Exactly," the neurologist said. "Those with a form of dementia may exhibit characteristic changes in thinking, day-to-day functions, and behavior shifts."

Pastor remained quiet until the neurologist finished talking and then he abruptly stood. "I do not have dementia or Alzheimer's," he said looking at each one of them, including the doctor. "Why you would bring me here for something so ridiculous as this is beyond me, Josie. Sure, I forget some things, doctor." He focused back on the doctor. "But I'm seventy-two years old. I've earned the right to forget. I have a lot that's circulated through this mind during the years the good Lord has granted me to be here."

"You're exactly right, Mr. Graham. The diagnosis is determined by a number of collective factors, not just one symptom. But what often occurs is signs of dementia may be more obvious to family members or friends. People with memory loss or other possible warning signs of Alzheimer's may find it hard to recognize they have a problem and may resist following up on their symptoms. We don't want that to happen to you, if we happen to determine that dementia is what you do have."

"I don't want to be a stubborn mule," Pastor stated and laughed. "I want to keep living the best life possible. I don't want to be a burden on anyone, especially my darling wife."

"Oh, Chauncey, you can never be a burden on me, but

we're here because like you, I want you to live your best
life, and I want to live mine too. No matter what this turns
out to be, I'm here for you. We signed up to be together 'til
death do us part, and I'm praying that the good Lord isn't
done with either of us yet."

The doctor and Stiles smiled.

"Well, Mr. Graham, I think you and your wife have said
it all. Take this paper to the front desk on your way out,
and the receptionist will schedule your next appointment.
I want to see you back here in a month. We'll discuss your
test results and I should also have your medical history and
files from your primary care physician."

Pastor reached for Josie's hand, helped her to stand, and
then turned toward the door. "Thank you, doctor." After
Josie stood, Pastor turned back around and extended his
hand to shake the doctor's hand.

"Have a good day," the doctor said.

Stiles walked up on Josie just as she stood in the entrance
of the kitchen. He reached out to her and she stepped into his
arms while he hugged her tightly. "Don't be afraid, Josie.
Pastor's as stubborn as a mule. He's going to be fine."

Still being held in Stiles' arms, Josie said, "I know, but
it worries me when he forgets things; simple things, too,
then on the other hand he can remember stuff that happened
years ago, like when your mother, when Audrey was alive.
And when he called me Audrey it darn near broke my heart.
That's when I knew something wasn't right."

She stepped back and out of his arms after accepting
his loving hug of comfort. It felt good to have someone

to confide in, to tell all about her fears for her husband's wellbeing.

"I'm so sorry, Josie. You know he wouldn't hurt you." He watched as tears formed in Josie's eyes and he felt deeply sad for her. He, too, was worried about Pastor. He prayed it was stress that caused Pastor's behavior change.

While talking, Josie got a plate, bowl and silverware, uncovered the containers of food that still sat on the stove, and opened them one by one, piling food on Stiles' plate.

She got another bowl out of the cabinet and put several big spoonfuls of apple cobbler in the bowl with lots of crust, which she knew Stiles loved best. She put the food inside the microwave.

"Your father is a good man. That's why I pray every day that Hezekiah will forgive him and just talk to him. I know it has to be hard on him, finding out the way he did about Pastor being his father. It was hard on all of us, but I just wish he would forgive Pastor."

The microwave buzzed and Josie removed the food and placed the plate on the table in front of Stiles. Next, she put the bowl of cobbler inside the microwave.

"We have to keep petitioning God."

"Yes, and I do," Josie replied. "We all make mistakes. As long as we're on this earth we're going to make 'em and we're going to keep making 'em. That's why the good Lord had to send his son to die."

"As a man of God, I'm just hoping against hope that Hezekiah remembers that to be forgiven he has to first forgive."

Chapter 17

"Sometimes I just can't ignore the way I feel when I see you smile." Unknown

Fancy sat on her usual row at Holy Rock. When Khalil told her Stiles would be rendering the message, she got up extra early, dressed, and darted out for the eight o'clock service. She hadn't had the opportunity to see him since he arrived in Memphis several days ago. She understood that he had more important things to do, see, and places to go while he was on this short visit, but she still wanted to make it her business to see him before he left to return to Houston later that day.

Today's message was about seeing the unseen. Stiles based his message on Hebrews 11:1. *Now faith is the substance of things hoped for, the evidence of things not seen.* "We're taught early on if you didn't see it, then you shouldn't believe it, but God wants us to do the opposite. He tells us in Mark eleven twenty-four, whatever you ask for in prayer believe that you have received it, and it will be yours. The key is to believe before you receive. You have to call those things that are not as though they are. Do not listen to the ways of this secular, materialistic, I have to see it first world we live in today. Put your faith into action. Do not fret; do not fear. Do not be anxious about anything," Stiles preached.

Fancy listened intently. There were times it appeared that Stiles was preaching to her. She felt like she was the only person in the crowded sanctuary.

By the end of the service, Fancy was standing on her feet, shouting and praising God. She was not alone, it appeared almost half of the people in the sanctuary and choir stand were shouting.

"That was an awesome message," she told him as she walked with him to her office.

"Thank you."

Fancy and Stiles arrived at her office door. She unlocked the door with the key she held in her hand. Stiles opened the door, extended his left hand for her to walk inside the office, and then closed the door behind them. Moments later, there was a knock on the door.

"Come in," she said.

It was Khalil. "Man, you were on fire this morning. Thank you for that word. We all needed to hear that."

The two men embraced tightly and then Xavier appeared.

Much like his brother, he praised Stiles for delivering a grand message. "You made it so simple. It was plain enough for a child to understand," Xavier said.

"The Word of God should be delivered where the least of those, from children to adults, can understand. I'm grateful the good Lord used me to do that."

"He surely used you," said Fancy. "I still feel the spirit."

"I give God the glory, not me."

"By the way, I didn't see Pastor Graham and his wife," Khalil said.

"That's right. I didn't see them either," Fancy co-signed.

"Yeah, I know. They planned on being here but Josie woke up with fever, chills, and a sore throat. Pastor wasn't about to leave her alone, so I said my goodbyes to them before I left the house this morning. Oh, by the way, could you send them a copy of the message. I promised them I would be sure to ask."

"That's understandable, and sure we can make sure they get a copy," Fancy said.

"Look, I'm going to jet off to the Youth Center. I'll talk to you guys later. See you, Mom."

"Okay, honey. I'll talk to you later."

"Later, Xavier," Stiles said.

"See you soon," said Xavier as he walked out of Fancy's office.

"Stiles, would you like to get a bite to eat before you leave? We can stop at Cracker Barrel since it's on the way to the airport."

"As much as I'd like to, I can't. You know how crowded Cracker Barrel always is, especially on weekends, and I have to drop off the rental car. I really won't have time to stop and eat."

Fancy's smile quickly faded. She wanted to spend some time with Stiles alone, but realizing that wasn't going to be the case, it dampened her spirit-filled mood.

"Sure, I understand."

"Yeah, of course we understand," Khalil said, turning toward his mother. "Ma, y'all can hang out on his next trip. Right, Stiles?"

"Yeah, no doubt."

Xavier returned with three DVDs in hand and gave them to Stiles. "Here you go. I thought I'd run down and get copies of the message so you'd have them before you left. I had them make three just in case you wanted one to keep for yourself, and for anyone else you might want to gift with one. Now I've got to get out of here. I'll be in the Youth Center for a while. See you, Stiles."

"See you, Xavier, and thanks." Stiles hugged his young nephew and then Khalil again before finally turning to Fancy and giving her a deep embrace followed by a kiss on top of her coiffed natural head of hair.

Khalil felt a sense of satisfaction that Stiles had to strike out. He noticed the look of excitement on his mother's face when she thought that she was going to spend time with his uncle. *Not today, Ma. Not today.*

Chapter 18

"The only journey is the journey within." Rainer Rilke

Fancy woke up, stretched, yawned, and climbed from underneath the soft, fluffy covers. Her new queen-sized bed with the sleep-pedic mattress made her sleep like a baby.

After taking a relaxing bath, she got dressed and ready for today's events. She was going to stay away from Holy Rock today—at least that was her plan—and have her some 'me time.' First, she went downstairs, following the aroma of fresh brewed coffee from her timed coffeemaker. Her coffee mug sat next to the brewer. She sat at the kitchen island and drank the piping hot brew while thinking about how she regretted not being able to spend time with Stiles.

Maybe she would take a trip to Houston. Of course, it wouldn't be to see Stiles per say, but she would go there because, from what she heard, there was so much to do. She wanted to visit Osteen's church. She would let Stiles know when she was coming and maybe they could hang out together, have lunch, dinner, or both.

She shook her head as if trying to pull herself away from that crazy thought. Aloud, she told herself, "Girl, you are not going to Houston. That man is your brother-in-law, your sons' uncle. Erase any ridiculous notions of the two of you becoming an item out of your head."

After she finished her coffee and erased thoughts of Stiles out of her mind, she brushed her teeth again to erase any signs of coffee breath, styled her hair, and then prepared to leave the house.

The first half of the morning she spent at the gym working out, something she hadn't done in ages. Next, she treated herself to a light but late breakfast at Brother Juniper's Restaurant.

That's where she saw him---or he saw her. The gentleman walked up to her table as she dined alone. She was scrolling through her phone, on social media, Instagram, and passing the time until the server brought her Portobello mushroom and red pepper omelet. She told herself she could splurge today since she'd just had a strenuous workout. It wasn't often that she came to this quaint but busy restaurant. She couldn't control her tastebuds because the food was so delicious. In addition to the omelet, she went all out and ordered a serving of cinnamon roll pancakes with hot maple syrup.

"Excuse me," the handsome gentleman said as he positioned himself in front of her. He had a slight smile on his face, a dark melanin complexion that complimented his clean-shaven skin, with eyes that were compelling and magnetic. If she had to guess, he was probably an even six feet, maybe a half inch shorter, with a sinewy build. He appeared to be in his mid-forties—it was hard to tell. His jeans, red multi-check shirt, and suit jacket made him appear rather distinguished looking. She glanced quickly down at his feet. His brown loafers were on point and she could smell a faint scent of his cologne, but the aroma of the delicious smelling food drowned it out.

"Yes?" she said, hoping she didn't sound stuck up or bougie, but she was curious about what he wanted.

"I wanted to compliment you on your hair. It's beautiful," he said. She touched her thick natural, curly locs of hair and smiled.

"Thank you," Fancy replied.

"I hope I'm not being presumptuous, but are you dining alone?"

"Uh, yes, I am. Why?"

"I'd like to join you, treat you to breakfast."

Fancy's first thought was to immediately tell the handsome stranger, no, but then she thought *why not? What could it hurt?*

"I'm Winston. Winston Washington," he said, extending his hand while waiting on Fancy's response.

She accepted his hand and his shake was firm but not overpowering. She liked that.

"Sure," she said.

Winston sat down across from her in the booth. "Thank you for allowing me to share the pleasure of your company."

"You don't know if it's going to be pleasurable yet," Fancy said and gingerly laughed.

The sound of his laughter was just as enticing as his baritone voice. It demanded attention and exuded sex appeal.

"Do you dine here often?"

"No, not really, only if and when I'm on this side of town and I want to blow off all the hard work I've done in the gym," she said, laughing more.

When the server brought Fancy's food to the table, Winston asked her if she would have his server to bring his order to Fancy's table as well. The server agreed.

"How do you like the food?" he asked.

"Oh, it's the best. This place is noted as being one of the best breakfast restaurants in the country."

"I didn't know that. It's my first time here."

"Is that right?"

"Yes. I live in a condo nearby. I moved here from Seattle a few weeks ago. I'm still getting settled in actually."

Fancy nodded. "I see."

The server brought Winston's food to the table. "See we already have something in common. I ordered the cinnamon roll pancakes, too."

"They're to die for," Fancy said, trying to suppress a giggle.

Fancy eyed his plate. He had a veggie sausage scrambler, cinnamon roll pancakes, cheese grits with butter, and a Juniper latte.

Hefty appetite. Must not have anyone at home cooking for him.

"Shall we bless our food before we devour it?" he said humbly, which right away impressed Fancy.

"Yes, certainly." She bowed her head. Winston reached over to where one hand laid on the table. He gently grabbed hold of it, bowed his head, and said a short prayer.

"Amen," he said and lifted his head.

Fancy followed. "Amen."

"Now let's see if Brother Juniper lives up to his name and reputation." His smile deepened into laughter and he put a forkful of veggie scrambler into his mouth.

Fancy watched him as she put a forkful of pancakes into hers. "Ummm, heaven."

His lips were full, perfectly shaped. His whole face spread into a smile as he chewed his food. "Heaven is right.

The best veggie scrambler I've tasted since I left Seattle."

"Uh, you said you just left Seattle a few weeks ago."

"Exactly," he responded and gave her a smile that caught her off guard and sent her pulses racing. Fancy brought up her hand to stifle her giggles.

"Wait until you taste these cakes."

Fancy and Winston enjoyed breakfast laughing and talking like they'd known each other forever. By the time they were done with breakfast and sipping on lattes and coffee, Fancy learned quite a bit about the mysterious Winston Washington.

He told her he had been divorced five years, had one grown son who remained in Seattle. He relocated to Memphis after his job as a top executive for a well-known tech company sent him to spearhead the opening of a brand new facility.

Fancy had heard of the company from the news. It was going to be a huge asset to the city by bringing in hundreds of jobs.

"That's great, Winston. I hope you like the city."

"So far, I do. Meeting you is the icing on the cake, and of course learning about these delicious cinnamon roll pancakes."

"Told ya."

"Yes, you did. So, Fancy McCoy. By the way, I love the name. It suits you perfectly. You're divorced too, huh?"

Fancy cleared her throat. *Here goes. The personal questions*, she thought. "Not quite. My divorce won't be final until a couple of months."

"I see. Any children?"

"Yes, two adult sons. My oldest son is senior pastor for a prominent church here in Memphis. Holy Rock Ministries."

"Is that right? I'm glad you mentioned that because I've been searching for a good church home. In Seattle I was a deacon. I also served on the New Members' ministry."

"Oh, you would love Holy Rock, that is, if you aren't intimidated by a huge church. Some people prefer smaller congregations, but we have a roll of over 8,000 members and it's continuing to grow."

"Now that's impressive. And so you know, very little, if anything intimidates me, Fancy." His eyes clung to hers, analyzing her reaction.

Fancy looked away. Winston Washington was captivating.

They finished the last of their beverages. When the server brought the check, Winston paid for Fancy's and left a generous tip.

Fancy was further impressed with this stranger.

"Thank you for the pleasure of your company, Fancy." They stood to their feet. He allowed her to walk in front of him and she led him to the exit.

Winston opened the door and they stood outside in the warmth of the clear, sunny spring day.

"I hope this won't be the last time I see you."

"You can always visit Holy Rock." She rummaged through her purse, retrieved her business card holder, opened it, and pulled out one of her cards. She passed it to Winston and he read it.

"Oh, so you're the first lady?"

"I *was* the first lady. Before my son took on the role of senior pastor, my husband held that title. Or should I say, soon to be ex-husband. He's no longer at the church. I still work closely with my sons."

"Understood. Well, I'd love to visit. Maybe I'll come

out," he looked at the card again, noting the times of the services on the card, "for Bible study one Wednesday evening."

"That would be great. I'll be sure to keep an eye out for you."

"Could I have your number, you know just in case I get lost."

There goes that smile again, Fancy said to herself and shifting nervously from one foot to the other.

"You can always rely on GPS," she replied and smiled. "And the church's number is on the card, too."

"You're going to make it hard for me, I see."

"No, that is not my intent." She paused, gazed at him for a second, and then said, "Here's my number." Winston pulled his phone off his side and began entering the number into his Contacts. When he was done, he pushed the Send button and Fancy's phone began ringing inside her purse.

"You can save my number, too," Winston suggested.

"Sure, or were you just trying to see if I actually gave you the right number?"

"That too," Winston said. "Thanks for allowing me to join you, Fancy."

"I had a good time," she told him as he walked beside her until she stopped at her car.

"This you?"

"Yes." She unlocked the car with her FOB and Winston opened the door.

"Thank you, Winston. Have a good rest of the day."

"You too. Looking forward to seeing you again soon."

"Yes, Wednesday night, seven o'clock, Bible study. Don't forget," she urged.

"I'll put it in my calendar as soon as I get to my car."

"Oh, one more thing," Fancy said as she sat in the driver's seat. "We provide dinner at five-thirty, if you'd like to come to that before Bible Study."

"I'll keep that in mind." Winston nodded, and then turned and walked off. Fancy sat in her car watching him as he strolled off before she turned the ignition and drove out of the parking lot. Her morning had started off great. She smiled along the way as she headed to her next stop—the Galleria to get her shop on.

Chapter 19

"Your eyes make me shy." Anais Nin

"Khalil, thank you. The flowers are beautiful," Eliana said, beaming with happiness, but remaining absolutely motionless for a moment.

"I still owe you lunch or dinner—your choice, or both." Khalil said, his eyes sharp and assessing—his voice deep and sensual.

"But why?" Eliana asked.

"It's Administrative Professionals' Day. As your boss I'm supposed to show you how much I appreciate you. Right?"

Eliana blushed. "But you do that. You always tell me what a great job I'm doing. You buy me lunch, and today, when those flowers came, I…well, let's just say you've done more than enough, Khalil. Really, you have."

"Nope, gotta do more," Khalil insisted. "So what's it going to be? Lunch or dinner?"

"You must have forgotten?"

"Forgotten what?" Khalil said, looking at her curiously, while checking out how beautiful she was.

"You and some of the other staff are supposed to be taking the admins to lunch today in recognition of Administrative Professional's Day."

"Oh, yea, right, right. Cool. But that's with the group. I want to show you personally how much I appreciate all you do to keep things straight around here."

"In that case and since you insist, it'll have to be dinner."

"Okay, dinner it is. Tonight? Say around six. Will you be hungry again by that time?"

"Sure. I leave here this afternoon at four-thirty. I'll run home, get dressed, and then I can meet you wherever you say."

"Nope," Khalil said, standing, walking from behind his desk. He perched on the end of his desk and folded his arms.

"Nope? What do you mean?"

"I'm picking you up. No driving for you. Plus, where I plan to take you is going to be a surprise. So, we'll go to lunch with the staff and this evening it's all about you...and me," he added.

"Ohhkay," Eliana said, surprised by this unpredictable man, but loving it at the same time.

Lunch with the staff and other admins went off without a hitch. Even Sista Mavis was on her best behavior, having recently celebrated her 60th birthday. Thanks to Eliana, Khalil had brought a small gift of appreciation for all the admins, and an extra gift for Sista Mavis to honor her birthday. She was feeling herself after that special show of attention.

Khalil eyed Eliana with obvious satisfaction. She was always on top of things and he loved that about her. She kept him on his game and things like what she'd pulled off today made him think how he wanted to spend some time, lots of time, with her outside of Holy Rock. He had been taking things extra slow, but now he was ready to step up his game. Tonight was the night he was going to pull out all

stops. He planned to wine, dine, and romance Eliana until
she was ready to melt into his arms. Of course, he wasn't
going to take her to his bed tonight—at least he didn't think
he would. That would come later, but it was definitely part
of his plan.

During lunch his text notifier sounded. He glanced at
his phone. It was Dee. Why did she always seem to text or
call him at the most inopportune times?

Hav a donation for the tv ministry, the
text read. Your place or mine?

Finishing lunch with staff. See you in
an hour, was Khalil's response.

I thought we could meet up tonight?

Tonight's not good.

Ok. Whatever. Guess I'll hold off on
this donation til you do hav time.

Khalil knew what that meant. She wanted him to
answer to her on her terms. For now, he was all about the
Benjamin's.

It'll be late.

Never too late when it comes to you.
See you tonight.

He closed his text down, not bothering to respond. He
would have dinner with Eliana and afterward he would go
to Dee's house to knock her off and get his money. Simple
as that, but if things went the way he expected them to go
with Eliana, Dee would soon be a thing of the past. Until
then, he would get as much money as he could out of her
to get a better than great start on the television ministry.
He still hadn't touched much of the money he stole from
his father. That was his stash that he planned to use only
when necessary. Holy Rock was paying him bank, paying

the mortgage on his new house, the lease on his Tesla Roadster, and many other perks. He had no need to hit his own stash when he was making a killing being a pastor. What a wonderful life.

Eliana stood outside The Italian Kitchen—a five star restaurant that boasted some of the best cuisine in the city. It would cost her a pretty penny just for a house salad, so because of that, she hadn't visited the fine dining establishment. A blank, amazed, and shaken look of surprise siphoned the blood from her face. When she asked Khalil where they were going, he refused to tell her, but thank God he admitted he was taking her somewhere fancy. She was glad he at least told her that much so she would dress appropriately, but fine dining was an understatement for this place.

"What is it? You don't like Italian?" Khalil asked, noticing her look.

"No, it's not that. It's perfect, Khalil. I've always wanted to eat here, but, oh, my gosh." She covered her face with her hands.

Khalil placed his hand on her back and guided her into the restaurant. The maître d' met them as they entered the warm and inviting space.

"Reservations, sir?"

"Yes, McCoy," Khalil stated, with his flat hand remaining on the small of Eliana's back.

This was more than she ever expected. Here she was, with Khalil McCoy, Senior Pastor of Holy Rock. This is what she envisioned, prayed about, and now she was here—with him. This was only the beginning she told herself as the two of them were led to a secluded section of the lavish restaurant to their fully set table for two. Everything was high class, exquisitely decorated.

"I don't believe I've told you how beautiful you look this evening, Eliana," Khalil said in the tone of a smooth talking, ladies' man. He meant every word. Eliana was a gorgeous girl. Her smile made him melt. The shape of her lips, the way she wore her hair, the way she walked, talked—he didn't have one complaint. And the dress she had on tonight accented her curves. She was perfect in every way. *The kind of girl I can bring home to Ma*, he thought staring at her from across the table.

"You've only told me about ten times since you picked me up," Eliana giggled. She was glad she had chosen to wear the black floral midi-A line dress with the floral square neckline. It wasn't too over the top and didn't reveal too much. She wanted to leave a lot for Khalil's imagination.

It was no secret that he was or had been a playa. There were women constantly calling Holy Rock and asking to speak to him. She had to field his calls like he was POTUS. Women showed up at the church, or bombarded him as much as possible at the end of Sunday and Wednesday night services. She couldn't blame them. Khalil was as fine as they come. Added to that, his voice, the way he could say the simplest things and make them sound like he was paying a lady the highest compliment. He was thoughtful, considerate, and observant. He noticed if she changed her hairstyle, wore a new outfit to work or a new fragrance. The man was on his game.

Tonight was no different. They would talk from time

to time at church. She'd told him things she didn't expect him to remember, like the fact she loved Italian food. And now, booyahhh, like magic, here they were, at one of the most top-rated, most-expensive, most exquisite Italian restaurants in the city of Memphis.

Khalil spared no expense and Eliana was well aware that he didn't from the prices on the menu. They dined on scallops, followed by primi and secondi dishes that included potato gnocchi, agnolotti, pork loin, and Saratoga. It was absolutely divine.

"This night means more to me than I can put into words," Eliana told Khalil as they came to the end of their three-hour dinner. Sipping on a cocktail, she felt herself become more at ease. She occasionally had a social drink, and tonight's dining experience with Khalil was ranked as a social event, so she indulged when the server offered her a cocktail.

Khalil chose lemon water and she felt a little uncomfortable, but he assured her it was no problem if she had a cocktail.

"I want this evening to be one you will remember for a long time." He looked at her as if he was photographing her with his eyes.

Eliana stared wordlessly across at him, her heart pounding. She could feel the sexual magnetism that made him so self-confident. Every time his gaze met hers her heart turned over in response. Her feelings for him were intensifying. It would be so easy to fall in love with Khalil McCoy.

"Well, Pastor Khalil McCoy, if that was your goal, then you have far surpassed yourself."

Chapter 20

"We are easily fooled by that which we love." Moliere

When they arrived at Eliana's apartment complex and passed Xavier's apartment Xavier and Ian were getting out of Xavier's car with boxes of pizza in their hands. Xavier lived on the first drive leading toward Eliana's street.

Khalil pulled up on the two of them. "What's up, bruh?"

Xavier appeared a little stunned when the car pulled up next to him, but then realized that there was only one guy in the city, his brother, who drove a whip like this one.

"Not a lot. About to dig into these pizzas," Xavier said, holding a large pizza with Ian holding two.

"Hey, brother," Eliana said with a huge smile covering her face.

"Hey, sis."

Ian looked and listened as his twin confided to him her strong feelings for Khalil. He warned her to keep her eyes open, guard her heart, and be careful. From what Xavier told him, Pastor Khalil was not the kind to commit. He was all about what a woman could do for him. Ian passed this info to his sister. What she chose to do with it was on her, but if anyone asked him, he would say she was too good for Khalil.

"Well, knock yourselves out," Khalil said.

"We'll talk later," Eliana told her brother and Khalil drove off.

Parked in front of her apartment, Khalil got out of the car and walked around to the passenger side to escort Eliana. He walked her upstairs to her apartment. "I hope you enjoyed yourself this evening."

"I did. It was perfect and I can't thank you enough." She noticed him watching her intently and longed to have him kiss her and be crushed by his embrace.

Khalil was no fool. He knew women. Since he was a young boy in the streets, hanging with older heads, he learned their ways by watching how the old heads got next to the females. With his good looks, his street smarts, and his fat pockets, he was able to pull the ladies at an early age. With time, he only got better. This role as pastor made it even easier.

He took hold of Eliana's hand. She anticipated his kiss, and Khalil could sense that she was totally into him. He leaned in and kissed her gingerly on her cheek.

It may only have been a cheek kiss, but it sent the pit of her stomach into a wild swirl.

"Goodnight. See you tomorrow."

"Goodnight, Khalil." Eliana removed the key from her purse, unlocked the door, opened it, and then turned and looked at Khalil as if inviting him inside.

He could have easily followed her cue, but he played a different hand, waited until she closed the door, and then walked off.

"She's upstairs," Priscilla told him when she answered the door.

He walked inside, closing the front door behind him. "Thanks, Priscilla. How are you?"

"Good. Thank you for asking." She feigned a smile, turned, and walked away.

Khalil shrugged, "Hey, baby," Dee said when he appeared at her bedroom door.

"What's up, Dee? He flashed a broad smile that turned into a rousing laughter when he saw her and what surrounded her on the bed. Shaking his head, he started undressing. "I see you got a package for me, yea? It's right on time. I can make the final payment. You are something else, Dee. Always on time."

"That's why you keep coming back," she told him as she lay naked on the bed with mostly hundred dollar bills spread over the sheets and on her. "Now hurry up and get in this bed. I've missed you."

Khalil shook his head. One thing about this *whatever it was* he had with Dee, dealing with her was full of perks and bonuses. Tonight was no different. After restraining his desires to take Eliana into his arms and make love to her, he used Dee to extinguish his penned up sexual release.

Fully undressed, he pounced in the bed next to her and on top of the money. He moved his mouth over hers, devouring its softness.

The caress of his lips on her mouth and along her body set her aflame. His lips were hard and searching. Dee answered his kisses with a gasp as he lowered his body on hers.

Fantasies of being with Eliana made it easy for him to make love to Dee as his body imprisoned hers.

Chapter 21

"It is through disappointment that I must learn to never accept defeat, but to always come up with a brand new plan and find a solution." Eleesha

"How was your trip?" Kareena asked.

"I guess you can say things were good. The meeting with the trustees and Khalil was productive. They offered me a lot if I accept the position."

"So, does that mean you're going to accept it?" she asked as they talked over lunch at one of the restaurants close to Full of Grace.

"If I do, it will be because of my father."

"Oh, that's right. He had the appointment with the neurologist while you were there."

"Yeah, I was glad Khalil adjusted our meeting when I told him I was coming to town for Pastor's doctor's appointment."

"How did that go?"

"I'm worried about him. I saw firsthand what Josie's talking about. His memory comes and goes and his temperament can go from mild mannered to being inpatient and on edge. Did I tell you he's even called her by my mother's name?"

"Oh, Stiles, I'm so sorry," she said, reaching out across the table. "I will keep him, and your family, in my prayers. I've never had any experience around someone who has dementia. Thank God."

"We don't know for sure if it's Alzheimer's. The neurologist did a series of tests. He has to return next month, so I'll be flying, maybe driving, back to Memphis for that. I can't let Josie go through this alone."

"That's understandable." They ate a few bites of their sandwiches before returning to address the elephant in the room.

"Look, it sounds like you're leaning toward accepting Pastor Khalil's offer."

"Why do you say that?" Stiles looked up from his food and stared into Kareena's eyes. He could sense that she was uneasy with the conversation, but she was right. He was seriously thinking about returning to Memphis. Like Khalil stressed, he wouldn't have to give up his pastorship in Houston. He could very well effectively do both.

"I say that because what you just said. Your father and stepmother need you. It's not like you'll be giving up your position here. They're going to pay you to travel back and forth, and you won't be required to preach too often. Sounds like the perfect second gig," she said, casting her eyes downward.

"I know, and you're right. It all sounds perfect. And the money isn't bad either. They're offering me a nice package. But if everything is so perfect, why am I so hesitant about accepting?"

"Maybe because of the memories of Memphis, Holy Rock, and fear. You experienced a lot of heartache and pain back there. It's understandable that you would be apprehensive. But if God is leading you to do this, then I think I know you well enough to know that you want to follow His will."

His tight expression relaxed into a smile. "You think you know me, huh?"

"Yeah, I do," was Kareena's soft mannered response. Each time they talked about this, Kareena felt a separation was taking place. They were no longer intimate, hadn't been for almost a year, but she still felt like this was the beginning of a break up. She could sense that his heart was being led back to Memphis. She didn't know if he had met someone while he was there or if it was like he said, because of his father's suspected illness. What she did know was that the distance between them was widening. It was time she took matters into her own hands if there was any hope of her salvaging the tiny cracks occurring in her heart.

"I have some exciting news," she said.

"Cool, what is it?" Stiles took another bite of his sandwich.

"River proposed."

Stiles coughed—his face turned into a mask of frustration.

She watched as a frown set into his features, followed by a bleak, tight-lipped smile. "When did this happen?"

"Actually, the night after you left."

"Yeah? I was only gone a few days. Wow, I don't know what to say. I mean, what did you say? Did you accept?"

"I did, but..."

"But what?"

Kareena couldn't hold back her feelings any longer. It was now or never. Before she gave her all to River, before she walked down the aisle, she had to know if there was any chance for her and Stiles to have a life together. She told herself after River proposed, she and Stiles should have talked things out, but she didn't want to ruin the relationship they already had. She admitted to herself that she was deeply in love with him, but she didn't believe he felt the same way. Today, no matter how painful it might be, she had to know how he felt.

"I love you." There, she'd said it.

The sound of silence sifted through the air as he contemplated the direction he should take. He did love her, maybe was even in love with her, but would knowing that be enough for him? It ranked low on the priorities ladder.

"Don't feel forced to say it back, Stiles. You've made it clear *many* times. I know there can be no future for us, *sooo* why would I think anything different now? I only told you that I'm in love with you because I wanted to hear myself admit it openly. Now I can move on with living the rest of my life."

He nodded, choosing to let silence do all the talking.

"I was in love with you, but that's not news to your ears. I slept with you, remember?"

"Have you slept with River?"

"I beg your pardon?"

"I said…have you slept with River?"

"What business is that of yours?"

"Just answer me, Kareena. Have you slept with the guy or not? It's a simple question that requires a yes or no answer?"

"How dare you try to turn this around and make this my fault." Her mouth dipped into a deep frown and a cold, congested expression settled over her face.

"I don't want to upset you, Kareena. Like I said, I care

deeply for you. I told you from the jump I wasn't ready for a serious relationship. I thought you understood that. So, I definitely understand that you have to do what you feel is best for you. If you're happy, then I'm ecstatic." His tone was indifferent, almost cold.

Inside, he felt bad as he watched Kareena fall apart from across the table. The last thing he ever wanted to do was hurt her, but he had no room to be in love. Not with all he had been through over the years. He resigned to believing that love for him was out of the question. He had needs too, sexual needs, and he tried to convince Kareena in the past that what they shared had been purely physical. He thought she understood. It hurt him to see how he had hurt her. He never wanted this to happen. He wanted the best for her, wanted her to be happy, to fall in love. But hearing her tell him that River proposed stung like a thousand bees on his heart. He had to convince her, even if it might hurt, that it was okay for her to marry River Garrett. River was one of the good guys. He could understand how quickly and easily he fell in love with Kareena, because she was easy to love.

"Yes, you're right, but I hoped, and prayed, you would let yourself fall in love again, but not just with any one, with me. I wanted to prove to you so badly that I would never hurt you." She gulped hard, hot tears sliding down her cheeks.

"Kareena, I'm sorry. Please don't cry. Believe me when I say, I'm sorry."

She tore away from the table and ran out of the restaurant.

Stiles was beyond sorry for what he allowed to happen. She was right. He knew all along Kareena was in love with him, but he still gave her false hope, something that he felt terrible about.

He left more than enough money on the table to cover the check and tip, told their server that he'd done so, and then hurried outside to find Kareena. He saw her standing at his car and he ran over to her. He tried to console her by grabbing her in an embrace, but she shoved him away.

"Just take me back to the church."

"Kareena, please. I'm sorry."

"You know what? It's not you. All this is my fault," she cried. "I should have listened to what you told me all along, but I prayed I could change your feelings. I hoped and prayed you would let me in. But you didn't and I have no one to blame but myself. Now, please, open the door and let me in the car."

Stiles did as she requested. Kareena got inside the car. Stiles closed the door and went to the driver's side. He got inside his car, turned the ignition, and in silence drove back to Full of Grace.

He had the answer to his prayer. He would accept Khalil's offer. It would give him some space, albeit, not total space, but space nonetheless, to gather himself and keep moving forward with his life. It would force Kareena to live her life and be with a man who Stiles believed deeply loved Kareena. From what he'd seen and heard of River Garret, he was the kind of man that would treat her the way she deserved to be treated, who would love her completely and unconditionally. Kareena deserved that and Stiles was not the man who was willing to give up his heart to do it.

Chapter 22

"The world is round and the place which may seem like the end may also be only the beginning." George Baker

"I'm planning a small dinner party next weekend, Xavier. I want you and your brother to be here."

"Ma, what will it look like with me and Khalil being at a party you're having? I mean, what would we do?"

"What are you saying exactly, Zay? Are you trying to call me old?" Fancy asked and broke into a wide smile.

"No, that's not what I'm saying...not really." Zay looked uncomfortable. He had stopped by his mother's office to discuss some questions he had about the youth ministry. She was always able to give him great advice and guidance when it came to that part of the ministry.

"Boy, don't be foolish. It's not like a real party party. It's a small intimate gathering to celebrate my upcoming divorce."

"Really, when it's all said and done, I don't have to hear from your father."

"What are you talking about?"

"I'm saying, my lawyer is handling everything. We don't have minor children and I don't want to be in a long and drawn out divorce battle. He doesn't want me then cool. I'm going to let it be. I'm not going to be one of those women who want to wallow in unnecessary drama. I want it over and done with."

"Yeah, but you could get something, Ma. You could find out about those bank accounts, what's in 'em, and any other assets he's hiding. You have to fight him."

"Nope. Don't wanna do it. Not going to do it. I already took all of the furniture, the house is sold, and it was in his name anyway, so I didn't contest that. Anyway, I prayed about it and decided the best thing to do is let it go and move on with my life. It's more about the principle. Like I was getting ready to tell you, my lawyer sent a car to take me to his office. When I arrived, we went over my decisions and I signed the divorce papers. Now all we have to do is go to court. That takes place a week from today."

"It's that simple, huh? After all the years you and Dad were together, it can be erased with the stroke of a pen. I'm sorry, Ma. I know this has to be hard for you."

"I'm fine. I'm a big girl. I'm a survivor. God has given me the strength to persevere through everything that's happened, and I will continue to stand."

Xavier walked over behind the desk where his mother was seated. He leaned down and gave her a tight hug.

Fancy patted him on the back of his hand. "Thank you, baby, but don't feel sorry for me. I'm not dead. There's plenty of life left in this forty-two year old body. Who knows, I might be able to pull a stepfather for you and Khalil."

"Ma? Stop it. But then again, whatever floats your boat. You are the most beautiful mother and woman in all the world, so I'm sure some of the men at Holy Rock have been secretly eyeing you. I won't be surprised when you start dating."

"Why, thank you, Zay. That's very nice of you. I've cried enough tears. It's time for me to start enjoying life again."

"Yep, fa sho."

"So, can I expect you and your brother to be at the divorce party?"

Xavier laughed. "Yeah, count me in, Ma."

"Good."

"Thanks for the advice about the youth ministry. I'm going to incorporate some of your ideas. You always have the best suggestions. If you don't need me, I'm going to leave early. I have plans later this afternoon."

"Umm, is that right? Is it one of the young ladies working with you on the youth ministry? I've seen a couple of them giving you the eye."

Xavier frowned. When would his mother and brother accept that he was not interested in any female?

He maintained his self-composure as best he could. "No, I made plans with Ian. I'm going with him to Nashville. I'll talk to ya later." He reached for the doorknob but Fancy in true Fancy fashion wasn't about to let the conversation die.

"Nashville? Right now? Don't you have to be at work tomorrow?"

"I already told Khalil that I wasn't coming in tomorrow. Ian has a meeting there tomorrow morning. He invited me to tag along."

Fancy didn't like what she was hearing, not at all. She had to hurry and put her plan into place.

"If he's going on business then what in the world are you doing going? Surely, you can't sit in on the meeting with him?"

"We're going to hang out when we get there and after

his meeting ends. I want to do some restaurant hopping, listen to some country music, oh and we're going to Green Hills Mall where all the name brand shops are."

"I still don't see why you have you go. If you wanted to go to Nashville, you and I can drive there any time. You are not his babysitter."

"No, I'm not. I'm his friend. No, I'm his partner, Ma, and I don't have time to get in a debate with you about my personal life. So, deal with it. Anyway, I gotta go. Thanks again for the help."

Xavier didn't give her the opportunity to respond. He walked out of the door, closing it behind him. Shaking his head as he went out the door, he didn't see Leo and he bumped into him.

"Oh, sorry, man," Xavier said. He hadn't talked to Leo since the day the man made a pass at him. On occasion, Leo worked with the youth too, but Xavier made sure he stayed as far away from him as possible. So far, until now, it had worked.

"How's it going?" Leo asked.

"Pretty good." Xavier continued walking up the hall and toward his office. Arriving in front of his door, he opened it and then looked at Leo who was standing there like he expected Xavier to invite him in. Not.

"Hey, do you have a minute? I need to talk to you about the sleep-in the youth are having this weekend." Leo asked just before Xavier closed his office door.

"I really don't, Brother Leo. You can talk to Sister Amy about that. She's overseeing the sleep-in."

"Yeah, I know, and that's what I want to talk about." Leo looked around like he was making sure no one else was in earshot. "I don't think she's the best choice. If you have a minute, I'll tell you why. I don't want anyone to overhear what I have to say."

Xavier exhaled. He didn't want to let the man in his office, but then again, he was the director of the youth department. If someone had issues or problems, he was the one they were supposed to come to. But he didn't exactly trust Leo's motives. Nonetheless, he opened up the door so Leo could come in.

"Okay, but I only have a minute. I have an outside meeting I can't be late for." Xavier made his point clear.

"Sure." Leo was about to close the door behind him.

"You can leave it open."

"I really think we need to close it. I don't want to take a chance of anyone overhearing what I have to say. Not until you have a chance to talk to Amy."

Xavier reluctantly nodded and Leo closed the door.

Leo went on to tell Xavier some crazy story about Amy hollering at the kids and the kids not liking her. Xavier didn't believe a word he said. The youth loved Amy. She was bubbly, friendly, and she was always planning great events for the youth ages thirteen to sixteen.

"I'll look into it. Thanks," Xavier said, sounding short.

Leo sensed Xavier's coldness.

"Look, Xavier. Let me say this, I'm sorry about that incident a few months ago. I was way out of line, but I think you took it the wrong way. Sometimes I get a little, well let's just say I apologize if I made you uncomfortable in anyway. I know you're gay and that's cool with me." Leo showed both palms while Xavier folded his arms together with a look of disdain plastered over his handsome face.

"Apology accepted," Xavier said. "Now, if you'll excuse me. I have to get ready for this meeting."

"Sure," Leo said. "Handshake?"

Xavier looked at Leo's outstretched hand. He didn't want to accept the shake but since the guy apologized, who was he not to accept it and let bygones be bygones. He extended his hand and Leo took it. He yanked hard, pulling Xavier against his aroused body with brute force. Xavier fought against him but Leo's grip proved stronger.

"What's wrong with you? Let go of me!" he shouted as Leo held him.

"You know you want it, "Leo snarled. "Come on, Xavier."

Xavier continued to fight against Leo. He managed to knee him in the groin with all of his strength. Leo abruptly released him and doubled over in agonizing pain.

"You little punk!" Leo yelped.

Xavier raced over to his office door, opened it, and then proceeded to push Leo out the door. "Get out of here and don't you ever come anywhere near me or I'll tell the whole bloody church what kind of pervert you are!" Xavier slammed the door so hard it sounded like it popped off its hinges.

Down the hall, Fancy ran out of her office from one end and Eliana thought she heard someone yelling, too. She got up from behind her desk and raced up the hall. Fancy's office was up the hallway and around the corner from Xavier's office but the thud she heard was loud enough for her to hear and send her running out of her office to see what was going on. When she saw Leo doubled over, she didn't know what to think. "Leo, are you all right?"

"Brother Leo," Eliana yelled next, and raced toward him. "What happened?"

"I'm okay," he said, forcing the words to come out

through the paralyzing pain coursing through his groin and radiating down his legs.

"I heard yelling."

Xavier opened his door back up. "You okay, Brother Leo? Sounded like you met the wall." Xavier stifled a satisfying smile and instead put a serious look on his face.

Leo glanced up at him and rolled his eyes and pursed his lips. With every word he forced, the pain magnified.

"Everything's good. Sorry about that," he said and rushed past Eliana until he was out of her view.

"What was that all about?" Sista Mavis walked up and asked.

Eliana shrugged. "I don't know," and returned to her workstation.

Fancy looked at Xavier with a look that said, *I know something just happened...and it involved you.* She turned and walked back into her office, closing the door behind her, while Xavier closed his door, locked it, and left the premises.

Xavier was outraged. On the drive to Nashville, he told Ian what happened. "The nerve of that prick."

"I'm glad you were able to fight him off. There's no telling what he would have done."

"Yeah, but I bet he'll think twice before he steps to me again. I kneed him as hard as I could."

"Are you going to report it to your brother or your mom? I think you should. That was sexual assault you know?"

"I stopped him. That's all that matters."

"Yeah, this time you were able to fight him off. What about the next time?"

"There better not be a next time." He had thought about it while he waited on Ian to swoop him up. His decision was final. He would keep this to himself like he did the first time Leo got out of line. It was the only choice he felt he had.

"Look, Xavier, I care about you. I don't want to see you get hurt. This Leo dude frightens me, man," Ian expressed.

"I can handle myself. I did today, didn't I?"

"Yeah, pretty much, but again, next time you may not be so lucky."

"I'm telling you, it's not worth running to my mother and my big brother. I really would look like a punk in their eyes. They'll say that I can't take care of myself. Well, I can, Ian. I'm a grown man. I can't run to my momma and brother every time I face a situation. This world is crazy, man. I know that, but I can handle it. Okay?"

"You sure you don't want me to talk to Eliana?"

"What! Are you crazy, man?" Xavier shouted.

"Chill out. It was just a suggestion. I won't say a word. What do you say we talk about something else?"

"Yeah, like how we're going to rock Music City tonight," Xavier replied, turning up the dial on the radio and moving to the music.

Chapter 23

"The happiness of your life depends upon the quality of your thoughts." Marcus Aurelius

After satisfying Dee by giving her what she wanted, Khalil placed the stacks of hundred dollar bills into the laptop case he had in his car. Dee said it was thirty-five thousand dollars. It was more than enough for him to close the television deal. She also gave him back the MasterCard Gold card, the one he'd thrown back in her face when he discovered that she was nothing but a trick going behind his back and meeting with that pervert George and his father. Since she insisted on returning the card, who was he to say no. She assured him that she had paid it off and that he could start afresh.

Before he left her bed the other night, he convinced her to tell him the last time she'd seen his father. Detria at first lied and said she hadn't talked to Hezekiah in ages, but knowing his father like he did, and knowing Detria, too, he knew that was a lie.

"If you want things to work out between us, you better start telling me the truth. No more lies."

She confessed that Hezekiah demanded she go with him to visit George in prison. George told her she was expected to look out for his needs by doing whatever he told her to do. She told him, after some added persuasion of a sexual nature by Khalil, that Hezekiah had moved first to an assisted nursing facility where he remained for a few short months, but had no idea where he moved to.

Khalil left Detria's bed in the wee hours of the morning. Now that he had what he wanted, he wouldn't have to return for quite some time, and he could put all his efforts into getting Eliana into his bed—an easy feat.

"Isabella, I want you to go to court with me. My divorce hearing is coming up in less than a week."

"But why?" she asked. She had no desire to be seen with him. She had to find a way of escape for her and her son, but she didn't know how she would do it. Hezekiah and George were two men she knew better than to cross. George threatened on more than one occasion to do something terrible to her little boy if she ever tried to run away or do anything to ruin Hezekiah or him.

She was glad when she was told George would be in prison for twenty-four months, but George's friend, Benny, could be just as bad, but Benny also kept her supplied with the drug of her choice. That was another reason she couldn't pull away from Hezekiah, she was heavy into drugs. There was nothing she wouldn't try. When she had her son, she prayed hard the kid wouldn't be born addicted to drugs because she managed to stop using, most of the time, after she found out she was pregnant. George changed all of that by sticking a needle in her arm days after she gave birth. Her addiction was once again full blown. As long as Hezekiah kept her supplied, she was not going anywhere.

"I want you there. Don't question me. Do you hear?" he yelled.

"Yeah, I hear you," Isabella answered.

"If anyone asks who you are, you're my caregiver."

"Okay. Whatever you say."

"Darn right...whatever I say. And don't you forget that." He turned around in his wheelchair and retreated to his room. "Fix me something to eat," he yelled.

Hezekiah retrieved his cell phone and made a call he hadn't made in months. Her cell phone rang.

When she saw the call came from an unknown number she ignored it. It rang again. She didn't answer—again. This time when it rang a local phone number appeared and she reluctantly answered, ready to blast one of those incessant telemarketers, and then again hoping that it was the guy from Brother Juniper's. She hadn't heard from him since their initial encounter. She scrolled through her phone where she'd saved his number under Contacts. Why she did that she didn't know. If it was him his name would appear unless he was calling from a different number. She told herself that he wasn't really interested in her in the first place. He was just being polite when he asked for her phone number. There were a few times she thought about calling him, but she still believed it was for the guy to call if he was interested.

"Hello."

"Fancy."

Fancy swallowed hard, flinching at the sound of his voice, and her face clouded with uneasiness. His pronunciation of her name was slurred but it was him.

"Fancy, how are you my...my luv?" He struggled to speak. Other than that, he sounded like himself.

She didn't know what she expected. She tried to sound stern but her stomach clenched tight, and she heard herself reply in a small, frightened voice. "Yes. What do you want?"

"I...mish...you. You m...mish.. me?"

"I don't have time for your games, Hezekiah. Do you realize how long it's been since I've talked to you? Since I've seen you? Now you want to call days before the divorce hearing. For what?" She found herself regaining her emotional strength. He was sadly mistaken if he thought a phone call would send her riveting back to that place, that place where her heart belonged solely to him. She wouldn't go there, would never go there again. Never would she allow him to walk over her and treat her like she was nothing.

"What do you want?" she seethed.

"Do...you...want a divorce?"

"This was your call but to answer your question, I think it's the best thing for us. You've shown me your true colors. At first, I wanted to blame it on your stroke, but that wasn't it. That wasn't it at all. You're a cheat. You didn't give a darn about me or your sons. Yes. I want this divorce. I want it more than anything I've ever wanted before." Her voice grew stronger as her thoughts raced dangerously. "Don't call me again, Hezekiah. I never thought I would say this, but I'm better, so much better without you. Goodbye!" she said, throwing words at him like stones before she ended the call.

She inhaled and then slowly exhaled. The phone rang again. She pushed the button without looking. "I said do not call me again!" She heard her bitterness spill over into the phone but she didn't care. "The nerve of that man," she said out loud.

"Whoa, hold up. Is this Fancy? Fancy McCoy?" the voice on the other end said in a resigned tone.

Realizing it was not Hezekiah, Fancy exhaled and then changed her tone. "Yes, this is Fancy. Who is this? How may I help you?"

"It's Winston. Winston Washington."

A soft gasp escaped. "Winston. What a pleasant surprise."

Chapter 24

"It is never too late to be what you might have been."
George Eliot

Filming started the first Sunday. Khalil was running around Holy Rock like the church was on fire.

"Settle down, Khalil. Everything is taken care of and in place," Fancy assured him.

"Yeah, man. You don't want to be showing how nervous you are on television, now do you?" Xavier said as Omar nodded in agreement.

"Omar, are you sure the cameras are in place and the colors we have on are cool?"

"Chill out. Didn't you just hear the first lady and your brother? Everything is going as it should. Now, get ready to go out of this office and deliver a powerful word. That's all your assignment requires. We got everything else handled."

Khalil exhaled, walked into his office bathroom, stood in the floor length mirror, and surveyed his distinguished signature attire of jeans, suit coat, and button up shirt. Once he was satisfied with his fashion he exited the bathroom.

"Let's do this," he said, looking at Fancy, Xavier, and Omar. Eliana appeared.

"Eliana," Khalil smiled. She looked sexy and beautiful

as always. He had to keep himself together, no time for his mind to start wandering down that lane.

"Good morning, Pastor Khalil. Good morning, First Lady, Xavier, Omar."

Each of the others said hello, but Fancy barely opened her mouth. Fancy eyed the young girl with a look of *I know you want my son but you have to go through me first since you haven't done what I asked you to do.* It wasn't that she didn't like Eliana, Ian was the problem. If that gay boy wasn't attached to Eliana, Fancy would feel differently, but because Eliana came with the baggage of her brother, Fancy decided she would have to see if there was a better match for Khalil. Being senior pastor of Holy Rock and now with this new television ministry, they didn't have any place for church gossip and rumors to start circulating about her sons—namely Xavier and that awful Ian.

Eliana arrived at Holy Rock bright and early to support Khalil on his big day. This television ministry was extremely important and she wanted to do whatever she could to help him be at ease and to assure that things went smoothly from an administrative end.

"Just checking to see if there's anything you need me to do before we go live. I'm so excited. God is really blessing Holy Rock—and you too, of course. You are the face of this ministry. And I should add, the mouthpiece too. You're going to lead thousands, no hundreds of thousands, to Christ through this ministry, Pastor. I'm claiming it!"

"Settle down, Eliana," Fancy stepped in between Eliana and Khalil and gave the girl a hard stare. "Look, thank you for your prayers and those strong words," and then she turned to face Khalil, "but we need to get to the sanctuary, honey. It's show time." Fancy turned, rolled her eyes at

Eliana, and strutted to the office door.

Omar trotted past her and opened the door. "You heard the first lady—show time." He stretched out a hand and did a half bow for everyone to walk past.

When they entered the sanctuary, Khalil felt another surge of excitement race through his body. This was a day he would forever remember. He could see the dollar signs and the endless numbers behind them. Yeah, this was going to line his pockets more than he could ever imagine and he was ready to collect.

The church was packed to overflow. This wasn't unusual, but today extra chairs lined the aisles, all three overflow rooms were filled to capacity and there was not a seat left in the balcony.

Xavier was positioned at the front of the sanctuary and took his usual seat across the aisle and to the left from where his mother always sat. He looked over his shoulder, people watching. People poured into the sanctuary. He saw Leo, his wife, and children enter and walk down the aisle a few rows to his right. Looking at that slime ball, no one would guess he was on the down low. He hated dude, and he wasn't going to let him get away with assaulting him. He just had to figure out what he was going to do and when.

Leo, without warning, met Xavier's eyes. He smiled and winked then turned to escort his wife to the church pew.

Xavier quickly looked away and turned his focus to the front of the church. "Bastard," he said underneath his breath.

Xavier remained in the sanctuary until right before Khalil approached the pulpit to deliver his message. He went to the finance office to monitor online giving and determine the amount of money Holy Rock would rake in during live Sunday broadcast.

As the donations began pouring in, particularly at the end of Khalil's message, Xavier was totally surprised. People were giving like crazy! "Pastor Khalil will be glad to see this," he said to one of the finance guys working alongside him. "Looks like we've struck gold! Holy Rock is on the map."

The other guys and women in the finance room began to cheer and praise God. It was wild. Xavier laughed.

Hezekiah sat up in his bed watching Holy Rock's broadcast. The choir had grown considerably, the sanctuary was filled to over capacity. As television cameras scanned the sanctuary, he saw his soon to be ex-wife and a lump formed in his throat. She looked good—real good. He caught a glimpse of his baby boy. He was totally disgusted by Xavier's admission of being gay.

"Got him working at Holy Rock when that boy should be shipped as far away from the church as possible," Hezekiah mouthed, talking to himself. "Number one mistake for you, Khalil. You don't need to surround yourself with the likes of your *wanna be a girl* brother. Then again, you're young and stupid yourself. Can't believe you would allow this either, Fancy."

Hezekiah was at home alone. Isabella had returned to Arlington to pack her and her child's clothes. He didn't send her alone; he had Benny to take her. He found and leased a small apartment in Piperton for her so she would be nearby. That way he could monitor her drug intake, and have her close by to help care for him.

He continued watching Holy Rock's broadcast until the credits rolled. Hearing his son preach caused him jealousy rather than making him proud.

Khalil and Fancy stole his ministry and the church from under him and he didn't see how he would ever forgive them. He called Fancy on the false pretense of missing her and wanting to see if she wanted to reconcile when he had no intention of doing so. When she practically bit off his head he had his answer—she was a bitter woman. He didn't see why she would be bitter when she was the one who wronged him. It wasn't his fault that she didn't put up a fuss about the house, cars, bank accounts, none of it being in her name. That was dumb on her part and now that their marriage was at an end, he was glad that she wasn't bright enough to demand they have joint accounts. "Stupid," he said aloud and laughed. "Stupid, stupid broad."

Khalil invited his mother, brother, Omar and his girl, and Eliana to a late lunch after the last church service. It was time to celebrate. The broadcast had gone better than expected with ratings through the roof, the television stations told him.

Xavier remained at Holy Rock to tabulate the money.

"Hey, what's it look like, Zay?"

"Man, you won't believe this. I told you before you left folks were giving, but I had no idea it was like this. It's crazy. Today's three offerings brought in six figures man, the television and social media giving is in the tens of thousands. I'm telling you, you're on fire."

"Thank you, Lord," Khalil almost screamed as he stumped his feet underneath the table and shook his head.

"We're in the m...we're blessed," he quickly changed his words.

"This is the first broadcast so I'm telling you, you should expect people's giving to increase. Look out, your love offerings are going to be outta this world, bruh. Shooot, I might need to start preaching." Xavier and Khalil laughed.

"Whoohoo, God is good. Okay, keep tabulating, Zay. We'll talk more later. I'm about to get my eat on. Oh, and Zay?"

"Yeah?"

"You got something coming, for real!" He ended the call and looked around at the table of people. "Order whatever you want! God's footing the tab today."

Fancy blinked, then focused her gaze. "What did Xavier say, honey? How did it go?" Fancy asked.

"Ma, let's just put it like this—you remember that verse, Proverbs uhhh, the one about the wealth of the wicked being stored up for the righteous?"

Fancy smiled. "Yes, that's in Proverbs."

"Well, let me put it this way," he said as he threw back his head and roared with laughter, "that wealth is being transferred as we speak."

Chapter 25

"A divorce is like an amputation: You survive it, but there's less of you." Margaret Atwood

Fancy left the courthouse sad and depressed. If Khalil and Xavier hadn't been there for support, she didn't think she would have been able to go through it. It was over in a matter of minutes. Seeing Hezekiah looking fine as ever caused part of her attitude. He may have still been in the wheelchair, but having gone without seeing him for months, she saw how much his health had improved. He was accompanied by a slender, no…skinny, model looking woman, who doted on him like he was a celebrity. She didn't know if it was supposed to be his caregiver or someone who Hezekiah was sleeping with. No matter who she was, it infuriated Fancy. How dare he bring some woman with him to court.

Fancy, he has to have help. He can't come out alone. Be for real. Those thoughts brought her back to some sense of reality, but she still felt extremely sad.

Her whole life, as she'd known it, had officially come to an end when the judge declared, "Divorce granted."

She didn't say one word to Hezekiah, not that he attempted to say anything to her or their sons. What had happened to Hezekiah? Was he like this all along and she had been too blind to see it? How could he be so cold and callous? He was dressed to the nines and he didn't seem to be missing out on anything other than being confined in a chair.

The judge didn't call either of them up to the bench, their lawyers handled everything. *Is this how it goes now? Is this all it takes?* Fancy thought again, fighting to keep back tears.

She watched as Khalil and Xavier followed behind Hezekiah, his lawyer, and the young woman as they exited the courtroom. She prayed they wouldn't cause a scene. The divorce was over and done with now. There was no need for words to be exchanged. All she wanted to do was get out of the courthouse and go home. She wanted this day, this moment, to end as quickly as possible.

Khalil got in front of Hezekiah's wheelchair, forcing him to stop, as Xavier stood at his side.

Hezekiah sat riveted and faced his sons while Fancy remained behind.

"So this is how it goes? No hello? No how you doing, sons? No sorry to our mother? Not even so much as a go to hell….nothing?"

Hezekiah remained quiet. He didn't have time for this crap. What did they expect him to say? Cheer them on for helping to ruin his life, his marriage?

In response, he raised his arm showing his gloved hand and the young woman behind his wheelchair began to push him.

"Excuse us," Hezekiah's lawyer said. "My client has nothing to say to you, personally. You can direct your questions or concerns to me."

"Cool, no problem," Khalil said and stepped to the side. "I don't have a thing to say to this buster but one thing. Your day is coming. Believe that." He glowered at his father before he and Xavier walked away while Hezekiah and his team continued toward the Handicap Exit.

Hezekiah held up a hand and the young woman stopped the chair. She turned the chair slightly so Hezekiah could get a view of his family. "Gimme my money, Khalil or you'll be sorry!" he yelled.

"Keep moving," the lawyer said.

The girl turned him back toward the exit at the instruction of the lawyer.

"Money? What money is he talking about?" Fancy asked. "The nerve of him. He's taken everything and now he's talking about he wants his money."

"Ignore him. He's talking out of his head. You crazy, old fool!" Xavier yelled at his dad.

"Just forget it. Let him go," Fancy said and began storming off in the opposite direction. "You see he's not the person we thought we knew. He doesn't care about us."

"Yeah, that was easy to see," Xavier said. "He's dead to me, Ma. I may as well not have a father."

Fancy heard the hurt in her baby boy's voice, and it caused her to hurt. But she imposed an iron clad control on herself. "Son, we're going to be fine. Life doesn't end because Hezekiah McCoy is no longer part of it."

"His day is coming," Xavier said, head lowered, he clenched his mouth tighter.

"You're right, Ma. We got this. We don't need him," Khalil said.

Since the divorce hearing, Fancy was in a deep dark place. Khalil and Xavier tried to comfort her by inviting her out to lunch or dinner, but she refused. She didn't go to Holy Rock, she refused to engage with her new women friends, and barely ate. She just couldn't seem to persuade herself to do anything. She needed time to wallow, to grieve over what once was. Maybe in time she would be able to take a step forward, but as for now, she didn't have the physical or mental fortitude.

Fancy was glad she allowed herself to branch out and start spending time with the two women. They were both around her age and in the Women's Ministry. Having other women to talk to, go shopping with, and share a meal or two, felt good and she'd come to enjoy their company. She invited them to the party and asked them to help her plan it. They stepped in and did a fantastic job.

Tonight was the party. Everything was in its place. Forty people out of the sixty she invited RSVP'd their attendance. Her new friends arrived early to help put the finishing touches on the decorations. The food was being prepared by a caterer one of them knew.

"This is going to be so much fun," Victoria said as she made sure the dessert table was arranged the way they talked about.

"I hope so. I'm so nervous. You know I'm not use to entertaining on this level."

"Yes you are, Fancy," Tara said. "The birthday dinner you gave Pastor Khalil was superb from the food to the entertainment, everything. We were just getting to know you back then, remember?"

"Yes, she's right, Fancy," Victoria said. "I don't know why you're so nervous."

"I guess because this is a different kind of party. I'm actually supposed to be celebrating…well, you all know."

Victoria threw up a hand, arranged something on the dessert table, while saying, "Look, you're going to be fine. I've had two or is it three divorce parties."

Tara eyed her up and down, looked over at Fancy, and the three of them erupted in laughter.

"You are so crazy," Tara said.

"You two keep me laughing," Fancy said as she walked to the other table where utensils, glasses, and other accessories were decoratively lined. "I don't know how I would have pulled this off without your help. I've been so depressed since I went to court."

"Anytime. I love doing stuff like this," Victoria said. "I'm glad we could help."

"So am I," Tara added. "Do you think we were going to let you lay around and have a self-pity party? Okay, so your marriage is over. I know it hurts. I was divorced too, but my life has changed for the better. I have a wonderful husband, a beautiful little stepdaughter, and we're expecting our own child in a few months." She massaged her growing belly. "God sent me someone better than my ex-husband during a time I thought my life was over. I was like you, depressed, crying all the time, could barely go to work. I almost got terminated, but thank God my manager, a wonderful woman, understood what I was going through."

"What Tara is saying is God has your back. He's not going to let you fall, Fancy. He's setting you up for something, maybe even someone, better. So, let's have fun tonight. Let's turn-up!"

Fancy couldn't do anything but laugh again. These were the kind of friends she'd always dreamed of having. Friends who stuck by her, who told her the truth, who wouldn't allow her to sulk and feel sorry for herself.

They looked around, surveying the tables to assure they were set up properly, then went into the kitchen, and then the large family room and living room where the guests would be. The weather was perfect and the backyard patio was decorated with chairs and tables for those who might want to enjoy the evening outside.

Fancy didn't tell her friends the other reason she was nervous about the party tonight had a name...Winston Washington. She invited Stiles but he told her he would be coming back to Memphis the following week for his father's test results so coming this weekend was out of the question. She was disappointed that he wouldn't be there, but when Winston called, she forgot all about Stiles Graham.

Initially, when she didn't hear from Winston, she chalked him up to being some random dude who had been blowing smoke up her nostrils with no intention of calling or seeing her again. Turns out she was wrong, and she was glad that she was. It may have taken him a minute to call, but once he did, the two of them talked and texted throughout the day. She felt like a school girl. He was able to take her mind off her problems and the reason she was throwing this party.

Chapter 26

"You can't start the next chapter of your life if you keep re-reading the last one." Unknown

The guests arrived and the party was going off without incident. Xavier, Ian, Eliana, Khalil, and the other guests mingled and enjoyed themselves.

Fancy had already talked to Victoria about introducing her daughter to Xavier. Victoria had seen Xavier at Holy Rock on many occasions but had never personally met the young man until a week or so ago, when she came to visit Fancy and Xavier was there.

Fancy told Victoria all about her handsome, smart, single baby boy, and arranged for Victoria's nineteen-year old daughter, Pepper, and Xavier to meet tonight. The one thing she purposely left out was Xavier's sexual orientation. Fancy believed all he needed was to meet a nice young lady, one that wasn't too stuck up, and Xavier would realize he wasn't gay after all.

Fancy met Pepper twice—once when she came to Holy Rock with her mother and again the week before when Pepper went with Fancy, Victoria, and Tara to shop for party items. The young lady had recently moved back with Victoria after having lived with her father and stepmother,

Victoria's first husband, in Texas. Now that she was a high school graduate and uninterested in attending college, Pepper was ready to step out on her own and move to Memphis where Victoria helped to secure her daughter a job at the same company where she was employed.

Fancy immediately received good vibes when she met Pepper. She appeared just as lively and lovely as her mother. She was funny, easy to talk to, and she'd had several boyfriends while attending high school. She learned that about her by simply engaging the young lady in conversation. Pepper was open, and Fancy discovered she had been quite popular in school. She had been a cheerleader since junior high and was just an all around, in her eyes, perfect girl. Her son would see the light. It would all start with their introduction tonight.

Khalil and Eliana talked and laughed almost the entire time they were at Fancy's party, other than the times Khalil had to put on his pastoral hat and mingle with the guests. He made his way toward his mother. He noticed she had been talking to the same strange man for quite some time. She had a glow about herself and a deep smile on her face as he watched the two of them. He approached them after having talked to several other guests and dismissing himself from Eliana.

"Excuse me," he said, as he walked up to his mother who looked like she was entranced by whatever the man was saying. Her eyes were glued solid to the guy.

"Oh, Winston, I'd like you to meet my oldest son, Pastor Khalil McCoy," Fancy said, looking at Khalil when he walked up. "Khalil, honey, this is a friend of mine— Winston Washington."

"Nice to meet you," Winston said, and extended his

hand and the men shook.

"So how long have you and my mother known each other?"

Fancy blushed. "We met at Brother Juniper's a few weeks ago."

Khalil nodded and said, "I see."

"Fancy tells me you're Senior Pastor at her church. You look rather young, but I know God calls who He calls."

"Yes, He does. Have you visited Holy Rock? I'm sure my mom has invited you since she's told you that I'm her pastor," Khalil said, testing the idea of his words.

Fancy caught herself glancing uneasily over Winston's shoulder and averted her stare from her son.

"Yes, indeed she has. We were just talking about that. I told her that I recently moved to Memphis, and I need to start looking for a place to worship. I have to tell you up front, Pastor Khalil, I'm not an every time the doors open kind of worshipper."

"I hear you, but my mother can vouch for me when I say I'm not the type of pastor that expects his members to be in the church pews each and every Sunday or whenever the church doors are open, although that would be ideal. I personally don't believe a person can get enough of hearing the word of God. But some people interact with our ministry through our new television broadcast. We also live stream our services too."

"Good, that leaves me without an excuse, huh? But the down side of not being there in person on Sundays, is I wouldn't be able to see your beautiful mother." Winston flashed a daring smile Fancy's way and she met his eyes as her breath caught in her throat.

"Well, if you'll excuse me, I'm going to talk to some of

the other guests. Great party, Ma."

"Thanks, honey. Enjoy yourself."

"The food is great. Ummm, and these mini Bundt cakes are delish!" Ian said to Xavier as they stood at the dessert table deciding what they would try next.

"Yeah, they are. I'm going to try this strawberry cupcake this go round."

"Excuse me, Xavier, sweetheart," Fancy said, touching her son on the back of his shoulder after excusing herself from the company of Winston. After all, she didn't want to hog all of the man's time and attention. That wasn't exactly the truth—she wanted to spend the entire evening with him. This was the first time she'd seen him since their initial encounter. He was more handsome than she remembered. But she had more important matters to tend to and that was to get her baby boy away from this little twit standing next to him and into the arms of a real woman.

"Hey, Ma," Xavier said and briefly hugged her.

"Hello, Mrs. McCoy."

"Hi," Fancy said curtly and then focused back on her son. Gently, but firmly, tugging on his elbow, she pulled Xavier away from the dessert table. "Sweetheart, come with me for just a second. There's someone I'd like you to meet."

"Okay, sure, Ma. I'll be right back, Ian. And, hey, don't eat all the strawberry cupcakes." He and Ian laughed as Fancy practically dragged him away.

"Who is it you want me to meet, Ma? It must be that man I've seen you hanging with most of the night. You've barely said a word to anyone else and this is *your* party, but hey, I'm not hatin'. I'm glad to see you smiling again."

"His name is Winston Washington. I met him a few weeks ago. I thought it would be nice to invite him. He seems nice enough, but that's not who I want you to meet right now."

"Then who is it?"

Fancy led him by his hand like he was still a little boy and she was walking him home from school. They weaved through the roomful of guests. Fancy and Xavier said a word or two as they passed. Music played, alternating between jazz, contemporary, Christian, and R&B.

"Where are you taking me, Ma?"

Fancy didn't say a word, except to Tara when Tara appeared next to her.

Holding a virgin strawberry daiquiri in her hand made at the cash bar, Tara giggled and whispered, "Hey, this is a great divorce party. We did this thang. High five!"

Fancy giggled and the two women gave each other high-fives.

"Where are you heading—outside?" Tara asked.

"Yes, aren't Victoria and Pepper out there?"

"Yeah, they are. That's where I was just coming from. I'm about to hit the food table. I'm hungry again," she said laughing.

"Okay, I'll see you a little later," Fancy told her and continued outside to the beautifully decorated patio.

She spotted Victoria seated at one of the tables talking to one of the single ministers from Holy Rock. He was cheesing all up in her face. Fancy had given Victoria a heads up about him. He was a widow, had a little money in his bank account, and was looking for a wife. Fancy was privy to a lot of personal information about members and staff of Holy Rock, which benefitted her in many ways.

"Excuse us," she said when she arrived at Victoria's table.

"Hey, Fancy. This party is great."

"It sure is, especially the company," the man said, smiling and looking at Victoria like she was his favorite meal.

"I'm glad you're enjoying yourself, Minister Davis. Victoria, where's Pepper?"

"She went to the ladies room. She'll be right back. Oh, look, here she comes."

Xavier leaned in and said to his mother, "Ma, what are you doing?" He slightly pulled away but she tightened her hold on him.

"I just want you to meet her, Xavier. For God's sake," she mumbled, "the girl isn't going to bite you. She just moved here, she's close to your age, and she doesn't know anyone. I thought you could at least show her around and you can introduce her to some of your friends in the youth ministry. Stop being such a sis..." She stopped herself.

Pepper walked up, "Hi, Mrs. McCoy." She looked at Xavier standing next to his mother, surveying every inch of him. "Hi." She broke into a smile.

Xavier's whole face spread into a wide smile. If he was attracted to women, she would be exactly the type of woman he would go for. Pepper was gorgeous. Her smile infectious and her voice articulate but light and friendly.

"Hi...Pepper?"

"Yep, that's my name...don't wear it out," she said and

laughed again.

Xavier laughed aloud. "Nice to meet you, Pepper. Xavier McCoy."

Fancy smiled. *This is going better than I expected. Look at my baby.*

"Well, now that you two have introduced yourselves, I'm going to talk to some of the other guests. You get to know each other."

Xavier looked at his mother, furrowed his eyebrows, but Fancy dashed off, leaving him alone to fend for himself with the beautiful, mysterious Pepper.

Chapter 27

"For every new relationship, there's at least another new broken heart. Ryan Barber

"What do you say we get out of here? I'm growing tired of playing the pastor role. You wit' me?"

Eliana looked up at him. She felt like a breathless girl of eighteen as his nearness made her senses spin. "Sure. Where are we going?"

"Anywhere other than here. Okay?"

"Okay, but what about my car? What am I going to do with it? I don't want to leave it parked on the street."

"Can't you get your brother to drive it back to your apartment? He rode here with my brother. If he can't do it, I'll talk to my mom. I'm sure she'll let you park it in her garage. If all else fails, I'll follow you to your spot and drop it off."

"No, I don't want you to ask her to do that. Let me go find him and I'll meet you outside."

"Okay, cool."

Khalil walked outside and looked to make sure his car hadn't been blocked in by any of the guests—it hadn't. He walked over to it, got inside, and while waiting on Eliana, he scrolled through his phone. There was the usual text from Dee telling him she wanted to see him. He shot her back a text, telling her he was at a function with his mother and would hit her back later. He saw a few calls from some other females he messed off with from time to time and then another few from some of the hungry females at Holy Rock who thought they could snag him by sending him naked photos. He shook his head and laughed at the thought.

He looked up and saw Eliana exiting the house. Her brother stood next to her. Khalil watched as she passed him a set of keys and pointed toward the street. He couldn't hear what they were saying, but assumed she was showing him where her car was parked. He nodded, said something to her, and she said something back before he walked back into the house.

"Ready?" Khalil asked as he hopped out of his car and went to the passenger side to open the door for her.

"I'm all yours," she said, hoping she didn't sound too eager.

You sure are, Khalil thought.

They sat in silence while Khalil drove toward downtown Memphis, along Riverside Boulevard, taking in the peacefulness of the nightlights lining the Mississippi Bridge.

"I'm glad we finally have some alone time. I've wanted to get to know more about the mysterious Eliana Hodges."

"Ummm, that's weird."

"Why do you say that?"

"Because I've wanted to get to know more about the mysterious Pastor Khalil McCoy," Eliana said shakier than she would have liked, but he was so very good looking, so sure of himself—she reacted strongly to him.

"Is that so?" There was a trace of laughter in his voice.

The pursuit of women like Eliana intrigued, motivated him, and made him want her even more.

"Yes, I know we learned a little about each other when you took me out to dinner, but there's still a lot more I'd like to learn about you."

"Same here. That's what this is all about."

Khalil drove to River Park and secured a parking space. Again, without speaking, he got out of the car, walked around to the other side, and opened the door for Eliana.

She didn't hesitate—she got out of the car as if she had been hypnotized. He reached out his hand and she accepted it as he led her on the winding walking trail on the Mississippi. There was a slight warm and gentle breeze. The stars, in all their majestic splendor, were on full display. There were a few other couples on the walkway or sitting cozily on the benches spread over the park. It was the perfect place for lovers.

They talked and learned more about each other than they had in all the past months since Eliana became his assistant. Laughter from both of them rang throughout the night and without warning, he kneaded her hand in his. She didn't pull away. It felt perfect; like this is where she belonged—beside Khalil McCoy.

Without pre-warning thunder clapped throughout the air, followed by a grand display of lightning that filtered through the sky.

Eliana jumped, frightened by the sudden sound. Khalil swung her into the circle of his arms and held her there. She buried her face against his throat, relaxing and sinking into the cushion of his embrace.

His hands explored the hollows of her back. Slowly, tenderly, and without words shared between them, Khalil lifted her chin upward, brushed a gentle kiss across her forehead, then the tip of her nose. She felt her knees weaken as his mouth swooped down to capture hers.

Another round of thunder, another lightning bolt decorated the sky like divine fireworks, but nothing could replace the fiery currents of desire racing through her.

Raising his mouth from hers, he gazed into her eyes as the first drops of rain began to fall. He smiled, took her hand, and they ran, laughing all the way to his car.

Ian walked into the living room looking for Xavier. He hadn't seen him for seen him for at least fifteen minutes. When he didn't see him in the living room, he walked into the family room where other guests were enjoying themselves. He wasn't there either so he made his way to the backyard. He didn't see him outside either. Where could he have gone? Maybe he was in the men's room.

After that assumption, Ian turned around to go back inside the house, but then he heard Xavier's familiar laughter. He stepped all the way out onto the patio, walked a few feet, and there to the right of him, shielded by a half wall was Xavier. He was laughing and talking to a young woman.

Ian watched for a few moments before he made the mental decision to interrupt what appeared to be an interesting conversation he and the girl were having. He was tired, had eaten too much, and was ready to call it a night, especially after he heard it thundering and lightning.

Several guests must have been thinking the same way because he saw them standing or moving about saying their goodbyes and preparing to leave.

"Excuse me, didn't meant to interrupt," Ian said.

Xavier turned around. "Oh, Ian. What's up? Pepper," Xavier turned back to face her, "this is Ian."

Bubbly Pepper replied, "Hi, Ian. Nice to meet you. So, is this your boyfriend?"

Xavier managed, after pausing, to say, "Uh, well, I don't think you—"

"We're just friends," Ian finished. "Look, it sounds like it's about to come down out here. Eliana left the party earlier with one of her friends. She asked me to drive her car home. You ready to bounce?"

Not giving Xavier room to reply, Pepper spoke up. "Hey, cool! You can take me home! It's not like I want to ride home with my mom, you know. And, hey, maybe we can stop over at your place so I can see that collection of African-American history books you were talking about."

"Good idea," Xavier said. "Hey, Ian, you can go on and bounce. We'll catch up later."

"Yeah, okay. See you...nice to meet you, Pepper." He gave Xavier an unpleasant glare before turning and walking off.

"Hold up, Pepper. I'll be right back."

"Sure. I'm going to go inside and grab something to eat. You want me to fix you a plate?"

"Uh, yeah. Thanks." Xavier darted off. He saw Ian going out the front door and followed him.

"Ian, hold up."

"What?" Ian said, sounding like he had a major attitude.

"You salty about me not leaving with you?"

"Naw, why should I be salty? You drove. You leave when you get ready."

Thunder clapped again. "Anyway, I'll holla. Enjoy the rest of your evening." With that, he jogged down the driveway and across the street to Eliana's car.

Xavier watched until he saw Ian approach the car. He shrugged and went back inside to find Pepper.

He found Pepper to be intriguing. She was down to earth and cool. At first he couldn't believe it when she came out and asked him if the rumor was true about him being gay. He was surprised she'd heard that about him because from what she told him she hadn't been in Memphis for that long.

He admitted to her without hesitation and without feeling weird that he was indeed gay. It was one of the few times he shared his preference openly with another person, afraid of being bullied or ridiculed.

"Okay, so you're gay. Who cares? You're sexy and fine, that's what I'm talkin' 'bout. And those eyes…boyyyy. Whooo." She broke out in soft laughter.

Xavier blushed at her openness while feeling surprisingly relaxed around Pepper. As they continued talking she told him about her love of reading and researching African American history.

Xavier was floored when she said that. It wasn't like he found many people in his circle, his very small circle that loved reading and learning about his ancestors. Pepper was able to share stories with him that he hadn't heard about, and his studies were extensive.

When he told her about his book collection, she was eager to see it, so tonight proved to be the perfect night. This was one of the reasons he was glad that he had his own spot. He could invite whomever he chose to, when he chose to, without his mother cowering over him to see who it was.

They hung out at Fancy's party for another hour. The rain hadn't fully started, but most of the guests had left.

"Mom, Xavier is going to drop me off at home," Pepper told her mother when they were getting ready to leave.

Victoria, standing next to Tara and her husband, smiled. The man who had been on Victoria's tail smiled too, like this was his lucky night.

"I'm going to go kiss my mother goodnight, then we can leave," Xavier said.

He looked around for his mother and found her outside with the same man who she'd been with during most of the party. He turned and left when he saw him lean down and kiss Fancy, and it wasn't one of those quick pecks on the lips. He kissed Fancy deeply, pulling her into his arms.

He thought about everything his mother had been through with his dad. She needed a little something or someone to make her smile and feel good about her life again. Maybe this guy would be that person. Turning on his heels, he strode up the foyer, there she was...

Chapter 28

"The meeting of two personalities is like the contact of two chemical substances: if there is any reaction, both are transformed." Carl Jung

All the guests had departed, except for one. "Thanks for coming," Fancy told Winston.

"Thanks for inviting me. I'm glad I came. It was fun. Not knowing many people other than my direct reports can make for a lonely man." He smiled and took hold of her hand as they stood at her front door.

She looked up at him with dreamy eyes and smiled. "We don't want you in Memphis lonely. If you decide to come to Holy Rock that will present another chance to meet people."

Thunder boomed and lightning cracked. The heaven finally released the flood of rain and it came pouring down in sheets.

"Whoa, I better get out of here," Winston said.

"Look, you have to drive across town and it looks horrible out there," Fancy said as they stood in the door looking out at the raging thunderstorm. Lightning continued to flash. Thunder seemed to roll across the skies in a deafening sound. "Why don't you spend the night?"

Winston released her hand and looked at her with eyes that blazed down at hers.

"In my guest room," she clarified. "There's only one requirement."

"And that is?" Winston replied, raising an eyebrow.

"You'll have to help me finish tidying up. There's not much at all to be done. My friends, Victoria and Tara, the ones you met tonight, did just about everything before they left, but I still have a few things I need to put away. Then we can settle in, have a glass of wine, maybe watch a movie."

"Or just talk. There's still a lot we've yet to learn about one another. But you have yourself a deal." He gave her a wink.

Fancy closed the front door and removed her hand from his.

Turning and walking to the family room, she smiled to herself. *Life without Hezekiah might be all right after all.*

Disregarding the storm that sent quarter sized hail knocking against the window, Xavier and Pepper pored over the pile of books he removed from his bookshelf.

"I can't believe you have all of these books about our ancestors, about the Mayans, and all kinds of African tribes and leaders. Do you have any in digital?"

"Yeah, but some of 'em were written so long ago and are out of print that I haven't been able to find them in digital."

"This is so cool, Xavier. Thanks for bringing me here. I can stay here forever going through this history of our people. There's so much to learn."

"I know, right. I'm glad you feel me. Not many of my friends or my family are that interested in reading about our history. If I tell 'em something I've learned or researched, they'll listen to that, but finding out for themselves...nah."

Xavier looked at Pepper with surprise, as she closed any space between them on the sofa. "I'm hungry," she said. "What you got in there to eat?"

"Not much of anything. I haven't gone grocery shopping yet. I was intending to bring food home from my mom's party, but I forgot."

"Yeah, that's probably my fault. You weren't expecting the change of plans."

"Change of plans? How is that your fault?"

"You and your sweetie, or whatever you call him, had plans of your own but then, boom, here I am."

"That's not your fault. I don't do anything I don't want to do. And Ian is *not* my sweetie. He and I are friends."

"Friends with benefits?"

"No, not that it's any of your business."

Pepper raised hands, got up off the sofa, and headed for the kitchen. Moving around like she had been there many times, she searched through the cabinets until she found a jar of peanut butter and a jar of strawberry jam. She looked on the counter and eyed a bread container, opened it, and removed a loaf of wheat bread.

"You want a PB&J sandwich?" she asked Xavier as he remained on the sofa, watching her.

"Sure," he replied, smiling.

"So, how long you and Ian been hanging out?" she asked while she prepared the sandwiches, loading each of them with a wallop of peanut butter followed by a wallop of strawberry jam.

"Couple months. What's up with the questions about me and Ian? Tell me about you."

"Okay, I moved to Memphis from Texas a couple months ago. Had a few boyfriends when I was there, none serious. I was a cheerleader from the time I was a little girl to the time I graduated high school. Went to community college for a quarter. Hated it. Dad said I needed to find something meaningful to do with my life, so I did. I moved to Memphis, started working at the same place where my mother works. Haven't met a guy yet. Let me change that. I hadn't met a guy yet—until you."

She pulled paper towels off the paper towel rack, placed the sandwiches on them and returned to the living room and flopped down next to him, reclaiming any space that could have existed between them. Kicking her shoes off, she curled her feet up on the couch next and snuggled under him as she passed him his sandwich and took a big bite out of hers.

"Oops, I forgot to get us something to drink." She hopped back off the sofa and went back to the kitchen.

"There's a carton of coconut milk in the fridge," Xavier said, admiring how she made herself totally at home in his apartment. It didn't bother him either. He loved how relaxed, comfortable and open she was with him. It made him at ease. If he could have a friend like Pepper, no strings attached, no expectations, but just a genuine friendship, then he was all for it. He'd never had a female friend before, but so far he found her to be cool.

"Okay, I see it. You want ice?"

"Ice? I don't think so."

"It's good with ice," she said and opened the freezer, got a few cubes out of the ice tray and put it in her glass.

Returning with two glasses of milk, she gave Xavier both of them, and he set them on the end table next to the sofa.

A bolt of lightning caused her to jump. "It's really coming down out there."

"Yeah, it is." Xavier took a bite of his sandwich and a swallow of his milk. "Here." He picked up her glass of ice milk and passed it to her.

"Thanks." She took a swallow and then offered him her glass.

"No thanks," Xavier said, pushing it away with a show of his palm.

"Try it. It's just milk with ice in it. Come on."

Xavier relented and tasted the ice milk. He tilted his head and raised his brow.

"See, I told you. It makes it taste even better."

"Yeah, maybe."

They continued going through the books while they ate.

"I'm sleepy," Pepper said.

"Come on, I'll take you home."

"No need. It's storming too bad out there. I'll stay here—if that's cool with you."

"Uh, well, okay. Why not?" This girl was full of endless surprises.

"Thanks. Point me to the bathroom. I'd like to take a shower."

"Uh, sure," he said, complete surprise on his face. Xavier stood. "Follow me. I'll get you some towels and one of my shirts."

"Thanks."

Xavier showed her to the bathroom, gave her some towels, and then left her in the bathroom. He returned shortly after with one of his shirts.

"Thanks, but I don't need it."

"What are you going to sleep in?" he asked.

"This," she said, turned on the shower, and dropped her towel without waiting on Xavier to leave. She stood there for a few seconds before she stepped in under the hot jets of water and began singing a Katy Perry song.

Her body was beautiful, perfect in every way. He tried to force himself to look away. He couldn't. What was going on with him? He began feeling something he had only felt with Raymone and Ian, but never around or with a girl. What was it about Pepper that was different? He listened as she sung before pulling himself together and walking out of the bathroom.

Xavier nervously paced the floor of his bedroom. This girl was one for the books. He sat on his bed and listened as she continued singing. She didn't have the best voice, and it made him laugh. He got up off the bed, went into the living room, and began putting away the books while she showered. He would sleep on the sofa and let her have his bed.

His cell phone rang just as he entered his bedroom to get a blanket and pillow out of his closet. It was Ian.

"I thought you woulda called when you got home." The tone of his voice revealed he was not pleased.

"I was intending to but—"

"Xavier!"

"Uh..."

"Who is that?" Ian asked. "Is that what's her name?"

"Xavier, the shower is all yours!"

"Yes, she's staying over. You know—because of the storm. Hello? Hello? Ian?" He removed the phone from his ear and saw that the call had ended. He called Ian back, but it went straight to voicemail. He called again and the message popped up *Call forwarded.*

His text notifier chimed. `You and her can both go to hell.`

"The bathroom's all yours," Pepper said again.

"Thanks." He turned, grabbed his robe, pajama bottoms, and went into the bathroom. While he showered he thought about how immature Ian had acted. Did he think that it was something up with him and Pepper? That was crazy. He would give him time to cool off and then call him tomorrow. Until then, like Pepper, he was exhausted and ready for sleep.

"Hey, you can sleep—," he saw her cuddled up in his bed, the covers pulled up to her neck, asleep.

He retreated to the living room, turned off the lights, laid on the sofa, and pulled the blanket over him. He didn't know how long he had been asleep when he was awakened by the weight of something on top of him. Dazed from having been abruptly pulled from his sleep, he was confused and frightened. What was going on? He opened his eyes and through the dark he barely saw her but he heard her childlike whimper.

"Come to bed with me," Pepper pleaded. "The storm is getting worse. Sounds like it's the end of the world."

Xavier eased up, his face inches from hers. She was right, the wind howled like an angry wolf, thunder raged, and lightning clapped. It sounded like a bunch of bulldozers were plowing through the apartment complex.

"Please, Xavier. I'm scared. Storms frighten me. I know I didn't tell you that, but they do. Just come to bed with me or I'll lay here next to you."

"It's not enough room for both of us," he mumbled.

She eased up and stood, taking hold of his hand when she did.

Reluctantly, he slowly got up and went to his bedroom with her. He stopped at his dresser, opened one of the drawers, and pulled out a polo shirt. "Here, put this on."

"Why?" she asked when he threw the shirt at her. "You don't like girls, remember so my being naked shouldn't bother you." She grinned. "Come on, get in the bed," she said just as another round of thunder and lightning filled the bedroom.

Pepper knew what she was doing. She could see that he was captivated by her nakedness. Gay or not gay, she was going to have Xavier McCoy. By the time she was done, he would be singing an entirely different tune.

Xavier climbed in bed, pulled the cover up, and shocking him again, Pepper snuggled her naked body against his bare chest, and wrapped her arm across him.

Her scent meshed with her naked skin against him physically aroused him and he was totally taken off guard by it. He turned over on his side, praying that she wouldn't be able to tell.

When he turned over on his side, she eased under his backside and nestled her head against him until she fell asleep.

Xavier lay on his side—eyes wide open.

Khalil and Eliana lay in his bed with her curled in

his arms. The evening was quiet discounting the fierce thunderstorm. He had put his phone on Sleep Mode so he wouldn't be disturbed by Dee's incessant texting and calling.

Eliana was a sweet girl but he saw through her sweetness a long time ago. She presented herself like a shy, demure girl at Holy Rock, but boy when he broke through her barrier, she was way different, and he liked it. He sensed from almost the beginning of them meeting each other that she liked him. He had that gift when it came to women. He could have made this night happen some time ago, but he played his hand carefully. He was glad that he had because he got exactly what he wanted—her in his bed.

He looked down at her as she hugged against him like a hand in glove. Pushing her hair back off her face, he leaned in and kissed her forehead, arousing her from her sleep, and making love to her again.

Chapter 29

"It is difficult to know at what moment love begins; it is less difficult to know that it has begun." Henry Wadsworth Longfellow

The following morning, the thunderstorm remained in full force. Fancy woke up early. It took a minute for her to recall last night's events. The party...Winston...

She popped up when she remembered he was a guest in her home. Dressing and grooming herself, she composed her thoughts and then exited her bedroom.

In the kitchen she began preparing breakfast. The night before she had laid out towels and a toothbrush in the guest bathroom. She hoped his sleep was pleasant.

While making breakfast and listening to the rain as it continued pounding on her rooftop, she began singing. *"Open the floodgates of heaven...let it rain,"* by Bishop Paul Morton.

"You have a beautiful voice," he said, startling her as he entered the kitchen.

"Thank you," she said. "How did you rest?"

"Great. It's still coming down out there, huh?"

"Yeah, it is. Would you like some coffee?"

"Yes, thank you. I can fix it. Just tell me which direction," he said, walking in her direction.

"Everything is over there at the coffee station. See," she said and pointed to her left at the coffee maker. Coffee mugs, cream, sugar, sweetener, everything needed to make coffee lined the area.

"Would you like a cup?" he offered as he walked over to the counter and poured himself a cup.

"No, I've had my one cup limit already." She giggled.

"I can drink coffee all day," he said.

"How do you like your eggs?" she asked.

"Soft scrambled."

"Okay, have a seat in the dining room and I'll be there in a minute."

"Let me help you," he said as he took a swallow of the hot brew before placing the cup on the island counter. He walked over and stood next to Fancy, watching her place food from the skillets and pots into bowls and plates. "What can I do?"

"You can take the food into the dining room."

"Gotcha." Winston carried plates of food to the dining room. "All this for the two of us?"

"Yep. I'm used to making enough for three hungry men, and I haven't learned how to downsize yet. I hope you have a big appetite."

"Oh, no worries about that. I do. It looks and smells delicious."

"No work on the weekends?" she asked as they returned to the kitchen, and Fancy passed him a pitcher of orange juice and a hot/cold container she'd filled with coffee.

The two of them sat at the table and like before, Winston prayed over the food before they began fixing their individual plates. Winston piled his plate with some of everything Fancy had cooked.

The dining room became quiet for several seconds while they indulged in the hearty breakfast.

By ten o'clock the rain had stopped and gave way to a cloudy sky.

"I guess I'll get outta here."

"I enjoyed the company. I'm used to having someone in the house. This house may be smaller, but I still haven't gotten used to living completely alone."

"I'm glad I could be here to keep you company," Winston said. "Come on, walk me to the door." He gently took hold of her hand and led her up the hallway into the foyer. They stopped at her door and Winston looked down at her. His gaze traveled the course of her face, searching her eyes. She couldn't deny the excitement building inside. She could feel his heart thudding against her own as his mouth hungrily moved over hers, parting her lips.

This is what she needed. As much as she wanted to tell herself no her body screamed yes as Winston gathered her against him.

He kissed her and without stopping walked her backwards until they were inside her bedroom. She looked up at him as she curled into the curve of his body. *Yes, one step closer.*

Chapter 30

"To have her here in bed with me, breathing on me, her hair in my mouth-- I count that something of a miracle." Henry Miller

Xavier woke up, looked around his room, but there was no sign of his overnight guest. He dragged his feet into the living room while rubbing the top of his head back and forth. He had very little sleep for more than a couple reasons. The storm that finally seemed to be letting up, had kept him awake most of the night, Pepper laying up against him was reason number two. The third reason was the one that he was most confused about—his physical arousal. He had never before been in bed with a woman, but he never had the desire to either. So why had his body reacted?

He walked into the living room and there she was. He looked at her like he was seeing her for the first time. She was an attractive woman. She was on the floor, sitting Indian Style, still dressed in the attire she wore when she entered the world with a pile of books around her and on the coffee table in front of her.

"Do you ever wear clothes?"

"Uh, not if I'm at home and there's no one around."

Xavier looked around the living room and then back at her.

"Okay, okay, I'll put on my clothes," she said. "Dang, I don't see why you're making it such a big deal."

She got up off the floor and started talking about one of the books she was particularly interested in while Xavier shuffled toward the kitchen.

"You'd be surprised at all the things that have been kept from us as a people. I'm telling you, reading those books is a real eye-opener."

"Yeah, for real though." She walked into the kitchen with the book in hand. "I ate a bowl of Cheerios. You definitely need to hit a grocery store, my friend." She laughed and gently popped him on the shoulder with the book.

The doorbell rang, catching them both off guard. She looked at Xavier and Xavier looked at her.

"Guess this will be a good time for me to get dressed," she said as Xavier left out of the kitchen and walked toward the door.

"I would think so," he said, shaking his head but not visibly upset. He understood that this was just who Pepper was. She was carefree and totally comfortable with who she was. It made him feel rather good that she felt comfortable enough around him to be herself. He hoped to be like that one day—not give two cents about what others thought, but he had a ways to go.

He looked back over his shoulder to make sure Pepper was gone and then he opened the door.

"I guess you turned your phone off since you had company last night," Ian said, storming into Xavier's apartment, flinging his hands in the air. "I've texted you God knows how many times this morning *and* I've called you at least five times."

"Oh, I guess my phone is dead. I forgot to put it on

charge last night. But hey, you're the one who hung up on me last night. I tried calling you back and you didn't answer. Now you want to come up in here this morning and go off on me."

"I didn't hang up on you. I thought you hung up on me. The phone must have died. Yours or mine, I don't know, but that was foul what you did last night, and all because of some girl. Man, what's up with you?"

"Xavier, you should get you somebody who won't be ready to slit your throat just because you don't report to him every minute of the day—or night," Pepper said, appearing in the doorway, still not fully dressed, but putting her dress over her head and then stepping into her shoes.

Ian turned three shades of red when he saw her come out of Xavier's bedroom. He looked at her like he could have chewed her up and spit her out and then gave Xavier a look that could kill.

"She's still here? You better have a good explanation."

Xavier was growing upset at Ian's behavior. He sounded on the verge of being abusive and Xavier didn't like that. He'd never seen the guy explode like this, and they weren't even in that kind of a relationship.

"Look, you need to calm down, man. I don't like the way you're coming at me. First of all, this is *my* apartment. I don't have to answer to anyone about who I have at my place. As for you and me, we've never established guidelines about a relationship. And truthfully, the way you're acting now, it makes me second guess us."

Ian started yelling and cussing.

"Look, you need to leave. Get yourself together and maybe we can talk later after you've calmed down." Xavier told Ian, trying to maintain his own self-composure.

Ian rolled his eyes at Pepper. She smiled and winked back without Xavier seeing her do so, and Ian stormed out the door.

"Um, that didn't go over too well," she said, giggling. "You wanna go get some breakfast now that the rain has let up? It's on me," she offered.

Xavier, again, shook his head in wonderment. "Yeah, I am hungry. Let me get dressed."

While they enjoyed breakfast together, Xavier expressed his sorrow about Ian and how he had hurt him. "I mean, Ian is a good guy. I really like him."

"When someone shows you who they really are, you should believe them," Pepper said. "That was not a good look on Ian. His behavior was way out of line. Dude came off like a mad man. You better watch out. This could turn out to be one of those crazy domestic situations."

"I don't think it'll go that far. I wouldn't let it anyway."

"You do a lot of reading, right?"

"Do you even have to ask me that? It's obvious." He took a bite of his waffle.

Pepper took a forkful of eggs, picked up her jellied toast, and popped the food in her mouth. "Look, I know you're gay, and I don't have a problem with who you sleep with. That's totally on you. But I like you, and I'd like us to be friends without someone like Ian going off every time we hang out."

"Yeah, I feel ya. I don't like that either, but I could have explained things a little better to him, so I won't put all the blame on him."

"I'm just saying, you don't owe him an explanation, and then again, I don't want to be the cause of friction between you and him."

"I got this. I can handle my own."

Pepper smiled, thinking to herself, *and so can I.*

Chapter 31

"I am not in the position to get hurt now that you love somebody else, because you were not mine in the first place."
Unknown

"Stiles, will you be coming home for Pastor's doctor's appointment next week?" Josie asked.

"Yes, ma'am. His appointment is Wednesday, right?"

"Yes, that's right."

"Ok, I'll be there. How are you two doing?"

"We're blessed and highly favored."

"Good. Where's Pastor?"

"He's in the den asleep on the couch.

"He's been taking his share of naps lately, huh?"

"Yes, he has. He used to say taking naps was for the lazy. All that's changed. He takes at least one, sometimes two a day."

"Listen, I'm praying for y'all. Call me if you need me."

"Okay, I will."

"I'll see you soon. Love you, Josie."

"I love you, too. Now go on and do what you need to be doing. Don't worry about us. I'll tell Pastor you called."

"Thanks. Goodnight." Stiles ended the call and his mind switched to his present situation between him and Kareena.

"The story of my life," Stiles whispered as he thought about Kareena and everything she'd said. How could she expect him to believe she was in love with him when she accepted River's proposal? If she really loved him she would not have accepted another man's marriage proposal. Stiles shook his head, pounded his fist on the desk, pushed back the chair and jumped up, causing the chair to topple over.

She wanted him to believe it was his fault. Yeah, maybe it was to a point, but she knew why he was the way he was. He had gone through some bad times, so had she, but not as bad as what he had experienced when it came to love and relationships.

Had he made the right decision? Placing his head in his hands, he pondered over what he'd done and what he hadn't done. It wasn't like he was moving out of Houston, giving up his church, or anything like that, but it sure felt like it.

He picked up the chair, set it back upright, and then sat back down. He reached for the phone lying on his desk, scrolled through the Contacts until he came to Khalil's number. Dialing him, he listened as the call connected and the phone began ringing. No answer. He let it ring until it went to Khalil's voicemail.

"Khalil, it's Stiles, man. I've made my decision. I accept your offer. Call me when you get this message."

Forty-five minutes later, Stiles heard his text notifier. He looked at his wrist and read the text message from Khalil. Hey, hey, give it up for Holy Rock's Assistant Pastor. Man, glad you accepted the position. I'm outta pocket right now, but let's talk later this evening and go over your official start date, and see about getting you a spot to lay your head when you're in Memphis.

Later that same evening, Stiles received a call from Khalil with Fancy on the other end, and surprisingly, Xavier was on the phone too. The three of them verbally extended him a round of congratulations.

"This is going to be cool, Stiles."

"Yes, God is good," Fancy added.

"Welcome back to Holy Rock," Xavier said.

"When do you plan on hitting the M-town?" Khalil asked.

"I'll be there in a couple weeks for Pastor's follow-up appointment. We can arrange to meet while I'm there, if that's cool."

"Yeah, that's straight. I'll email you the contract. Look over the salary and benefits."

"I hope you're pleased with what we're offering," Fancy spoke up.

Stiles smiled. It was good hearing her voice. She'd gone through a lot, and for a minute he was concerned about her mental state. When it came to the love she had for Hezekiah, she was weak. Stiles often thought about a woman having that same kind of love for him, but that was one less thing he needed to think about.

"I'm sure I'll be pleased, but I'll look for the contract, read over it, and we'll discuss it when I get there. Fancy, it's good hearing your voice."

"You, too, Stiles." She was happy that he would be back at Holy Rock, even though it was part-time. The fact that he was returning was what was good about the whole thing—period. Who knew why God was allowing him to return. Maybe he would be the one to break through his brother's impenetrable shell before there would be no turning back for Hezekiah. She quickly changed that pattern of thought. No one was beyond impenetrable, not for God. What was she thinking?

"Oh, Stiles, one more thing," Khalil said.

"What's that?" Stiles asked.

"Nothing major, just something Zay noticed. I remember you saying you were a couple years older than my father."

"Yeah, I may have mentioned that."

"Well, the three of us—me, Mom, and Zay were looking over your last contract."

"Yeah, your birthdate stood out," Xavier added.

"Why is that?" replied Stiles.

"Me and Zay were laughing about you being Dad's big brother."

"Yeah, I am."

"Actually, if Dad's birthdate is correct, it would make him the oldest."

Stiles frowned. "For real? I don't think so. I thought I distinctly remembered my birth mother saying I was the oldest. Then again, I don't know what to believe. Anyway, it doesn't matter; I don't have a relationship with him anyway and knowing your father, I'm sure he couldn't care less whether I'm older, younger, or not his brother at all. He'll never accept me either way."

"Hezekiah has abandoned us all, not just you," Fancy said. Stiles was sounding like he was a victim. He must have forgotten her family and what Hezekiah had put them through.

"I understand that. Believe me, I do. I'm just saying, with all I'm learning about my family, the more doubt I have about who I am, who my mother really is, *and* about my father. I don't know what's true, what happened, and what didn't happen. Anyway, thanks for telling me. That brings up another subject."

"Before you change the subject, I want to tell you, congratulations. We'll be glad to have you back. Now, go ahead and tell us what you were about to say."

"Thank you, Fancy."

"If you'll excuse me," said Xavier, "I have to hang up. I have a videoconference in ten minutes."

"Understood, talk to you later, Xavier."

"Okay, Stiles."

"Fancy and Khalil, I'm not going to hold you. I just wanted to ask if either of you've heard from Hezekiah."

Xavier disconnected from his end of the call and left his brother and mother to answer Stiles' probing questions.

Khalil answered the question. "Haven't seen that busta since he and Mom's divorce hearing. He thought he was gonna get away without saying anything to my mom, me, and my brother, but I had to confront him, tell him about himself. It didn't make a difference to him, but it's cool. Long as I got what I wanted to say off my chest. I can't believe a man like him raised me."

"Don't harbor bitterness in your heart, son," Stiles cautioned. "It keeps you from being all that God has called you to be, and you're a man of God. You have to learn to forgive." Stiles couldn't believe he'd spoken those words to Khalil. *Try practicing what you preach,* said the voice inside his head.

Chapter 32

"Don't look where you fall, but where you slipped."
African Proverb

Nine and half weeks had come and gone since Fancy and Hezekiah's divorce was finalized. Fancy still had bouts of momentary depression. Living alone was taking getting used to. She had come to enjoy having girlfriends. Victoria and Tara helped take her mind off the demise of her marriage.

Not being around Holy Rock every day of the week was another thing she had to get used to. Since Khalil was swiftly learning more about the inside operations of a church like Holy Rock, he didn't call on her as much. He and Xavier made her proud. Both of them had stepped up to the plate and the operation of the church was moving full speed ahead. The television ministry was booming, the congregation was growing, and the money was flowing.

It amazed Fancy at how mature and responsible her sons were. They were about their business. Dem McCoy boys were a force to be reckoned with and it made her proud to be their mother. Too bad their father was missing out on all this.

Fancy finished getting dressed for her date with Winston. They had been spending quite a bit of time together. Khalil and Xavier didn't question her much about Winston. All they wanted was to see her happy and enjoying life.

Winston was charming, a good conversationalist, and quite adventurous in and out of bed. He pushed her out of her comfort zone to try new things. They'd gone hiking and camping in Far Creek, Tennessee, something she never imagined she would do. They'd even gone to a Beyoncé concert, of all places. She was beside herself when he presented two lower level tickets to the concert in Nashville. He was always doing something to surprise her and she loved it.

He visited Holy Rock a couple times, but hadn't become a member. Fancy didn't push the issue because it was a personal decision he would have to make on his own.

Fancy wanted an easy relationship that allowed her to do what she wanted to do when she wanted to do it, without feeling the pressure of questions and explanations about her comings and goings. Since she had to start her life anew, it was not going to be the same as when she and Hezekiah were together. She stepped into her stilettos just as the doorbell chimed. She smiled, knowing it was Winston.

George, Detria, and Hezekiah, sat outside on the grounds of the Federal Prison. They purchased food from the commissary store and had something of a picnic. It was a hot day but not as hot as it could have been in the month of July. August would be upon them in another week and George was counting down the months before he would be outta this place.

"What do you have to tell us about the McCoys?" George questioned Detria.

Hezekiah looked sternly at her, waiting to hear what she had to say. She never seemed to have any relevant news to share. Either she was lying or Khalil was smarter than the average bear. He opted that it was more than likely the latter.

"There's nothing to tell." She was almost too high to speak clearly. "Y'all already know Khalil's television ministry is a success. He says he's raking in money hand over fist."

"How often do you go to church?" Hezekiah inquired.

"Not too often. You know the church scene isn't my focus."

"Yeah, your focus is on getting Khalil to walk you down the aisle. But a word of advice—if you plan on being first lady again, you'd better get on your hustle. You should be up in that place every chance you get," George urged.

"Not that it would make a difference. No way will my son ever marry someone like you. Let's be real," smiling wickedly, Hezekiah said almost clearly and with the slightest slur.

Detria rolled her eyes and appeared crushed. Was Hezekiah right? *Maybe I am being a fool for believing Khalil will marry me one day. He hasn't been coming over that much lately. But that's because he's busy. There's a lot to running a conglomerate like Holy Rock.*

"You're useless," Hezekiah said.

"Yeah," George countered, "what do you need her around for?"

"Good question, George."

She suddenly sounded sober for a minute. "Don't do this, Hezekiah. Where would I get my stuff?"

"A woman with as much money as you, I'm sure you'll find someone who'll supply you with as many drugs as your little heart desires. You get how much a year?"

Detria didn't open her mouth. She let her eyes do all the talking.

"You and that kid you never spend time with are set for life."

"I'll try to find out more. Just don't tell Benny to cut me off," she spoke up and pleaded like the dope fiend she was. "And keep my son out of this."

Hezekiah thought about the similarities between Detria and Isabella. They were actually two peas in a pod. Both dope fiends, both of them needy and insecure women. While Detria could have any and everything money could buy, Isabella was a down on her luck kinda girl. The difference was Isabella adored her kid and her drugs while Detria enjoyed her drugs *and* her drugs—oh and his son, Khalil.

"What's Winston been saying?" Hezekiah asked George, reverting his attention from glassy eyed Detria.

"He says she's feeling him. He's supposed to visit me tomorrow, but from what he says, your ex is giving it up like there's no tomorrow. He's handling his business, getting her just where he wants her. Soon, she'll be praying to the good Lord of hers to become the next Mrs. Washington." George reared his head back and laughed.

Hezekiah still felt some type of way hearing that another man was smashing his wife, but hey, Fancy had messed things up in their relationship. She deserved whatever Winston got out of her. When George came up with the idea of setting up his friend, Winston, to meet Fancy, Hezekiah balked at the idea at first. The more he thought about it, he began seeing that it would be just the thing he needed. He banked on Winston getting Fancy's gullible behind to fall in love with him, maybe even marry him if that's what he wanted, and then drag her ignorant behind through the mud while keeping Hezekiah in the loop about his family and Holy Rock. It would serve her right.

"What about Khalil?" Those thugs of yours screwed that up," Hezekiah said as Detria sat quietly in her own drugged out world.

"They scared him enough to make him move, so mission accomplished," George replied.

"Mission may be accomplished for you, not for me. I still don't have my money that boy stole, and I need my money. If I don't get it, then Miss Lady, you're going to have to hand it over out of your own personal stash. You got that?"

Detria answered with a show of silence.

"Did you hear me?" With his good strong hand, Hezekiah reached over and twisted her right arm until Detria screamed beneath her breath and tears shot from her eyes.

"Yea...ahhh, yes," she squealed.

"When I talk to you, I expect you to answer. You understand?" he yelled, still holding on to her arm.

She shook her head and looked around like she was looking for a prison guard who happened to be nowhere in sight.

Hezekiah released her, and snatched his hand away. "Now, like I was saying, I want my money."

"And you'll get your money back. Gimme some time.

I'm working from behind these steel bars, you know."

"Man, you doing gravy time in here. Look around you. This place looks like a luxury resort instead of a federal penitentiary. I bet they're plenty young boys you got your sights on in here." Hezekiah looked around the yard full of prisoners. "Probably got the pick of the litter up in here."

"Nah, it ain't like that. Believe me, it's a long way from being a resort. Anyway, I'm not done with that *thinks he so smart* eldest son of yours. Not by a long shot. He's going to get what's coming to him. He's going to give you your money back and then some. While we're on the subject of money, what about that other baby mama of yours? You heard from her? She sent out any more fake Wills lately?" George leaned back and laughed while Detria looked like she was zoned out in another world.

"You got jokes, huh. Anyway, nah. I don't know where she is with my kid, but at this point I have bigger fish to fry. She'll turn up sooner or later since she ain't getting money from me. I'm glad you brought her up too, 'cause I don't need her popping up on me with none of her drama. Know what I mean? Just like she sent Fancy that fake Will, she'll do anything. That fool is crazy. Let's just hope she stays ghost for a minute until you get out of this place. I'll decide what I'm going to do about her when the time comes. You feel me?"

"Humph," Detria said and looked off in the distance at some of the other men prisoners passing by.

"You got something to say?" Hezekiah turned and scowled at Detria.

"Huh, what?" Detria replied.

"Man, let her be. She in her own time and space. Benny got her feeling good, huh?"

Hezekiah and George both laughed. "Yeah, he does, and if she wanna keep feeling that good she betta get her act together," Hezekiah said and gave her an *if looks could kill* stare.

Chapter 33

"Oh, Khalil, they're beautiful." Eliana glowed, standing in his office behind closed doors. When the dozen red roses were delivered to her, though no note accompanied them, she immediately guessed they were from her boss, her pastor, and her lover.

"Beautiful roses for a beautiful lady," he told her, enveloping her in his arms and kissing her deeply. "And congratulations on becoming an official member of Holy Rock under the guidance of none other than Senior Pastor Khalil McCoy." He ravished her with more kisses. First, he kissed the tip of her nose, then her eyes, until finally, he satisfyingly kissed her soft mouth.

When she first joined the staff of Holy Rock she was a longtime, faithful member of her home church. Last Sunday, all that changed. She had to step up her game now that she was sleeping with Khalil. Becoming a member of Holy Rock would be a *win-win* and put her one step closer to the opportunity to become the first lady.

She could care less that his mother didn't seem to like her anymore for whatever reason. Initially, when she met

Fancy, the two of them hit it off, but slowly things changed. Eliana felt it was because she hadn't followed through with Fancy's request for her to find a girl for Xavier.

Eliana made up her mind she was not going to give the thought space in her mind when it came to Fancy, Xavier, or her brother. Her agenda was hooking Khalil. Their relationship had escalated since the night of Fancy's party.

Kahlil was feeling her and without question she was feeling him back. He may have had his underlying reasons for pursuing Eliana, but regardless of the reason, he thought she might make a good first lady. He'd had his share of women. Some silly immature girls and some older stupid and needy women like Dee. He smiled as he hugged and felt on Eliana at the thought of how gullible Dee was. This time he'd gotten what he needed, fully needed from her, but he still wasn't quite done. He could use her money and as long as she was willing to dish it out, he was going to make sure he was there to eat from her plate.

Xavier and Ian were civil toward one another—whenever they saw one another, but since the blow up between the two, Xavier maintained his distance. He didn't need or want any unnecessary attention drawn to his already colorful life.

He didn't try to put a lot of time into why he enjoyed Pepper's company so much. It was understandable the two of them had a lot in common. In his younger days he was a reserved type of kid, into his books, his grades, and of course back then he was into Raymone. He thought of Raymone often. A few weeks ago he'd heard that Raymone and his family had moved to Arizona. Something about it being more conducive for Raymone's health and the type of around the clock treatment he needed.

Xavier never had many friends, unlike his brother. Before meeting Pepper, he never had a single female friend that he could recall, but all that had changed. He and Pepper were thick as thieves. They hung out almost on a daily basis. They attended poetry readings, went to dinner, the movies, literary events, especially African American literary events. He found her easy to talk to, and she always kept him laughing.

"That was the best movie ever," Pepper exclaimed, grabbing hold of Xavier's hand as they left the movie theatre. "They say it's the highest grossing film in history."

"I can see why. It was mesmerizing," Xavier shot back.

Pepper stopped, gave him one of her crazy looks that Xavier had come to love seeing her make, and then she put both hands on her slender hips.

"Uh, did you say mesmerizing?"

"Yeah, what?" Xavier responded, looking back at her with his own weird look.

"You are such a nerd," she said, laughing. "Come on; let's go get something to eat. Do you mind if I stay over at your crib tonight?"

"When are you going to get your own spot, Pepper? Not that I mind you sleeping over, I'm just saying. If you don't like living with your mom, you've been working for a minute; can't you get a spot of your own?"

"Just tell me that you don't want me to spend the night. You don't have to go into all this other stuff." Pepper flailed both hands and walked ahead of Xavier.

He ran up and caught up to her. "Stop whining. Let's order a pizza and go to my apartment."

She looked at him and smiled, stood on her tiptoes, and pecked him lightly on his mouth.

They stopped, ordered two pizzas, an order of breadsticks, and a tray of double chocolate brownies. Afterwards, Xavier drove Pepper to her mother's house and she ran inside and retrieved several articles of clothing and accessories. He waited outside in his car, patiently.

Victoria had been keeping Fancy up-to-date with what she heard and saw going on between Pepper and Xavier.

Fancy couldn't be happier; she believed God for a miracle in her baby boy's life because that's exactly what she believed it would take to change him from gay to straight.

Pepper and Xavier sat up in his bed eating pizza, drinking soda, and munching on breadsticks and brownies while watching an episode of a new series they were following on Netflix.

"I've been thinking."

"Uh, uh. I know what that means," Xavier said as he popped a piece of gooey brownie into his mouth while sitting with the foot of his exposed legs propped up on a bed pillow. He was dressed down to his undershorts and of course, in true Pepper fashion, she was naked as a bird, well almost. She did have her panties on this time. Xavier was accustomed to her now and wasn't disturbed when she entered the apartment and began to immediately remove her clothing.

"No, I'm serious. It's been on my mind for a while. A long while."

"Oh, yeah. How long?"

"Since your mother's party."

"Wow, that was over two months ago. What can you possibly still be thinking about regarding her party? It wasn't that memorable. All it symbolized was the end of my mother's marriage. That's something I don't wanna dwell on. You know?"

"Yeah, but it's not about the party—it's about when I spent the night with you that first time. Remember?"

"Uh…yeah. What about it?"

"Okay, remember, we were in bed together. I was afraid of the storm so you came and slept with me."

"Yeah. I, uhhh, okay." Xavier stopped eating and looked into Pepper's eyes. "What about it?"

"Well, it was hard not to notice that you...you became aroused."

"No way. That didn't happen, Pepper."

"It *did*, Zay. I wouldn't lie about it. We've been hanging out for a minute. Well, since the night of the party, so I think you should at least be able to know enough about me to know I say what's on my mind and I have no reason to lie. You know I'm telling the truth. Anyway, let me ask you this. Have you ever been with a girl?"

Xavier turned a shade darker. "That's like me asking if you've ever been with a guy and if so how many."

"Yep, I've been with a guy. As for how many, I'd say quite a few. See how easy that was." She plopped another piece of pizza in her mouth and picked up her breadstick and took a bite of it.

"I'm not like you, Pepper. I don't talk about my personal life with people I just met. And contrary to what you say about us knowing one another, I can't say that I know much

about you. All I know is you like to run your mouth—
nonstop."

"See, you do know something about me," she said,
sounding unbothered by what could have been taken as a
scathing remark. "Stop avoiding the question, Zay. Have
you been with a woman before, or even laid next to one
before me?"

"None of your business. And again, I'm telling you to
lay off. I don't talk about my sex life."

Disregarding what he said, acting as if it didn't bother
her—because it didn't, she continued. "When did you know
you were gay?"

Xavier said nothing.

"Okay, do me a favor and I'll leave it alone. Hold up
first. Just a minute. Lemme go get my tablet out of my
purse." She got up off the bed, ran into the living room, and
came back with her tablet.

She turned it on and while waiting on it to power on, she
took a bite of the chocolate brownie. "Umm, these brownies
are sooo good!"

"What are you doing? I'm not looking at any sex pics."

"Boy, please," she said and laughed aloud. "Okay, here
it comes. Hold on just one more second. Here," she said
scooting in close to him and placing the tablet where they
both could see. "I want you to read this book, "Eternal
Victim Eternal Victor" by Donnie McClurkin. You may
have heard of him. He's a little old school now, but he's a
gospel preacher and singer. Had a lot of hit songs before we
came along and he was also a gay man."

"I've heard of him. But you said he *was* a gay man?
What do you mean, he *was*? And why do you want me to
read his book?"

"Just do me and you both a favor. Read the book. I think you'll learn a lot. There's something different about you, Xavier. Were you abused as a kid? I don't know why I sense that, but I do. You don't have to admit it, but you do need to admit it to yourself so you can move on—I mean if that's what happened."

"Just because someone is gay, it doesn't mean that person was abused or assaulted, Pepper. Where do you get all this stuff?"

Xavier hoped he hid his shock well. Pepper was such a different person from the people and friends in his life. She was young but she seemed far wiser and almost clairvoyant. How did she know that something happened to him when he was a kid? Was it that obvious? Was it written all over his face, or was it in his demeanor, his walk, his talk? He didn't want to think about the older boy who abused him when he was nine years old. He never told his parents, his brother, anyone. Now this girl sitting next to him had just called him out and it scared the bejesus out of him.

Chapter 34

"All at once everything is different--Now that I see you."
Lyrics from "I See the Light"

Stiles lay in his own bed, something he did very little of. He usually fell asleep on the couch in his man cave, but tonight was different. He shaved, showered, ate a sandwich, and got in his bed where he fell asleep while reading about claiming one's spiritual gifts. The phone startled him from his sleep.

"Stiles!" The hysterical woman on the other end of the phone said.

He sat up in his bed, rubbing sleep from his eyes, and looking around the dark bedroom trying to get his thoughts together. Was he dreaming? He looked at his hand and saw the name and number on the phone and brought it back up to his ear.

"Hello? Cynthia?"

"Stiles. Oh, my God, Stiles!"

"Cynthia, what is it? What's wrong?"

"It's Leo. I think someone tried to rob him. Whoever it was beat him up real bad," Cynthia cried. "He's in a coma. I...I know he'd want me to tell you," she continued wailing.

"When? Where?"

"Last night...rather more like after midnight—around two o'clock. Someone saw him...found him unconscious in an alley, downtown, next to—"

"Next to what, Cynthia?" Stiles pushed her to talk. He understood she was upset. Leo was her husband, the father of her children. She had every right to be more than upset—she had the right to be hysterical, and that she was.

"One of those clubs where homosexuals go."

"Have the police found who did it?"

"No, they're pulling the surveillance tape. Thank God the cameras were working and running."

"I'll try to catch a flight out of here as soon as I can."

"No. Leo wouldn't want you to do that. I'll call you when I learn something else."

"I'm supposed to be flying into Memphis in a few days anyway. But, listen, keep me updated. If I need to come now, I will."

"Okay, you know I will."

"Are you alone?"

"No, our next door neighbor is with me and some of mine and Leo's family members are here."

"Let's pray." He prayed for his best friend's healing while thinking, *Come on, Leo, man, not this again.*

Xavier and Khalil sat in Xavier's office discussing plans they put in motion to get back at their father.

"From what I've been able to learn, he should be under

indictment," Xavier told Khalil.

"Good, hopefully they'll pick his two dollar behind up, throw him behind bars in a cell with that pervert, George."

"*Oh, wouldn't that be lovely*," Xavier sang.

A knock at the door made them stop their conversation. "Come in," Xavier said.

"Excuse me, Pastor Khalil, Brother Xavier," Eliana said in her professional work voice.

"Yes, what is it, Eliana? We're almost done," Khalil said.

"I thought you would want to know a call came in from Cynthia Jones, Brother Leo Jones' wife. He was found unconscious late last night. He was badly beaten; he's in a coma. They don't know if he'll make it."

"Man, that's terrible. I'm really sorry to hear that. Have you notified any of the ministers on call to make sure someone is at the hospital?"

"Yes, two of the ministers are on the way there now. They may already be there."

"Good, thanks again, Eliana. Oh, and please send flowers from the chur—"

"I already did," she said before he could finish his sentence.

"And I've arranged for the Sick and Shut In Ministry to start preparing food for Cynthia and their kids, and arranging childcare so she can freely stay at the hospital as long as she needs or wants to. That'll be one less thing she'll have to worry about."

"You're the best, Eliana."

"Thank you, Pastor Khalil. I'll let you know if I hear anything else."

Khalil's eyes followed as she turned and closed the door.

Xavier clasped his hands together and smiled.

Three days later, his smile widened when Holy Rock received the news—Leo Jones died from his injuries.

"You seem rather happy," Pepper told Xavier as they went apartment hunting for her.

"I am. It's been a pretty good week. Added to it being a good week, you're out here looking for your own spot. I'm happy for ya." Xavier grabbed her around her shoulders as they walked up to the next leasing office for some apartments she'd read about online.

Xavier was still reveling over hearing the news about Leo. He was sorry for the grief his wife and children must have been experiencing, but as for his feelings, sad to say, he was almost ecstatic. Added to his death were the rumors circulating saying Leo Jones was on the down low and had been for years. Xavier wondered if Stiles knew about Leo since from what he heard the two men had been friends since back in the day. If Stiles said he didn't know about the dude, then Xavier didn't know if he would believe him or not. The typical person wouldn't wish death on another, and he hadn't wished that on Leo, but now that he was dead, Xavier didn't feel bad for him either. He was found in the alley of a well-known downtown club frequented by gay men and lesbian women. Zay was tempted to go to the club a time or two with Ian, but he never built up enough resolve to do so. He had a reputation to uphold and he didn't know if he could accept ridicule or victim shaming by judgmental people.

Leo's funeral would be in two days and Xavier had no plans to attend. If he did, it would be just long enough to make sure the man lying in the coffin was indeed Leo Jones.

"I like that apartment," Pepper said as they finished the tour of the model apartment.

"Would you like to put in an application?" the leasing agent asked as he walked along next to her and Xavier.

"Yes, I think I would."

"Good. Please come to my office and we'll get started."

Two weeks later, Pepper moved into her two-bedroom apartment located seven miles from Xavier. They bought two bottles of wine and some Chinese and went to her place to celebrate. By the end of the night, Xavier wasn't a drinker, so after finishing off a bottle of wine between the two of them, he was lit.

Sitting back on her brand new sofa, a gift from her dear mother, Pepper laid against his chest and listened to his breathing. He had fallen asleep. He sounded so peaceful. Being with him was always the highlight of her day or evening. That's how much she enjoyed his company.

Without waking him, she got up, went into her bedroom, removed her clothing, and took a shower.

"Pepper," she heard him calling. "Pepper, where you at?" he asked, still sounding inebriated.

Pepper laughed. "In here, silly. The bathroom."

Xavier barged into the bathroom, causing the door to hit the back of the closet on the other side.

"Watch what you're doing there. This is my first night here. I don't want to lose my deposit on my first night," she said laughing. "Come on, get in here with me."

"No thanks," Xavier said, sounding like he was sobering up after her invitation.

"Don't be scared," she teased. "I won't bite you, and I'm sure you could use a shower. Wash some of the stench of that wine off you."

Without forewarning, she took the soap in her hand and began washing his perfectly sculpted body. Xavier grabbed her hand when she began to reach intimate spots, but she didn't stop. His lack of resistance, scaring even him, turned into full unbridled desire when she continued washing him. She encircled her arms around his waist, closing any distance that might have existed between them.

On her tiptoes, almost slipping as the soapy water rendered her unsteady, Xavier grabbed her tiny waist and held on to her. Her lips found his and he did not turn away. He heard the sounds of desire and passion move from his groin up through his rib cage and out through his throat where a guttural sound poured out.

Being a virgin to a woman, he explored the newness of it all. The sensation ripping through him was like none he had ever experienced. His hand seared a path down her belly and onto her thigh as he explored before moving gently down the length of her back, her waist, her hips.

As she writhed against him, she drew her face to his, and pressed her open lips to his. He returned her kiss with a savage like one of his own as he became lost in the moment. The wine mixed with feelings he never thought about like this, took over and he was helpless to stop the need for her. Waves of ecstasy soared through them as they took their relationship to another level.

"Who is it?" Isabella asked as she was awakened from her sleep by loud, obtrusive knocking that also woke her son. The child began crying and calling for his mother.

"Now what?" Hezekiah asked, as he turned in the bed toward Isabella, lying next to him.

"Don't you hear that knocking? Who could it be?"

Hezekiah raised himself up in the bed and looked over at the clock. "Four-thirty in the morning! For God's sake, who is it? Get up and go see, and stop him from crying too."

Isabella got out the bed as fast as she could, grabbed her gown and put it over her head, followed by her robe. She ran into the other room and picked up her crying little boy, and tried to soothe him as she raced to the door.

"Open up!" the booming voice demanded.

"I'm coming. Hold on," she said, frightened about who could be demanding she open the door.

At the door, she looked through the peephole. "Who is it?"

"FBI," the man said. "Open up now."

"Hezekiah, they say it's the FBI," she yelled to Hezekiah who was in the room transferring himself from the bed to his chair.

Clad only in his undershorts, he made it to the door faster than he had been able to move since having the stroke.

"FBI! Open up!" the voice demanded again followed by more pounding.

Isabella opened the door. Four men almost barged inside. "We have an arrest warrant and search warrant for

Hezekiah McCoy," one of them said. "Are you Hezekiah McCoy?" one of them asked, looking at Hezekiah.

"Yes. You say you have an arrest warrant? For me? You must be mistaken. What is this about?"

"You've being charged with five counts of felony embezzlement. Hezekiah McCoy, you have the right to remain silent...."

To be continued in Book IX
Those Folks at Holy Rock
Winter 2018

Words from the Author

Each time I start another book in this series I keep thinking and saying to myself: *"This is it. This is the last one."* Yet, as I write, the more this story unfolds. The Grahams and the McCoys keep talking to me and they've told me that I'm not done until they say I'm done. Boy, do they have a lot to say.

These two families can teach us so much about living life. We see the good, the bad, and the ugly when it comes to the stories of their lives. The same holds true for each of us—we can never be certain what life will throw our way. Sometimes we find ourselves on top of the world and then the next minute or moment we can find ourselves at the bottom of the pit feeling lost, hopeless, and lonely.

Because life is unpredictable, I believe this is why we should always have an anchor. For me, that anchor is found in God and my faith. I'm not saying that my faith doesn't get a little shaky sometimes (okay, a lot of the time), but I believe if I can just hold on to faith the size of a tiny mustard seed that everything will be all right. So far, God has never failed me and even in my darkest of times, I am still here.

The Grahams and McCoys may be fictional characters, but they show how flawed we all are. It doesn't matter whether you stand in a pulpit and preach the Word of God, you are still flawed. It doesn't matter if you have the best of everything, you are still flawed. It doesn't matter if you are struggling or if you are living a life of ease- you are still flawed.

The important thing I want to continually remind you is that no matter who you are, no matter how you mess up, no matter how many mistakes you make, how many wrong turns you take, as long as you are living and breathing and the blood runs warm in your veins—things can work out. Have faith. Trust in God. Never give up.

Contact information
www.sheliaebell.net
www.sheliawritesbooks.com
sheliawritesbooks@yahoo.com
www.facebook.com/sheliawritesbooks
@sheliaebell (Twitter & Instagram)
@literacyrocks (Instagram)

Follow my Amazon author page bit.ly/sheliabell

Please join my mailing list
for literary updates and new book release information
www.sheliawritesbooks.com

If you enjoyed this book please go to your favorite review site and
leave a positive review!

Group Discussion Questions

1. What is your opinion about the Graham family versus the McCoys?

2. Do you believe Khalil McCoy is sincere about his call to the ministry? Why? Why not?

3. How do you feel about Fancy and Khalil McCoy's opinions about Xavier?

4. Should Xavier remain at Holy Rock or leave and pursue his life. Why? Why not?

5. What do you think about Stiles and his hang ups about love and about forgiveness?

6. What should Isabella do with her life?

7. What do you think Winston Washington is up to? Does he like Fancy or is he using her? Why? Why not?

8. Is Kareena right in moving forward with her life if she can't get Stiles to make a change? Why? Why not?

9. What do you think about the relationship between Xavier and Pepper?

10. What do you think about the relationship between Khalil and Eliana?

11. Did Leo get what he deserved? Why? Why not?

Perfect stories about imperfect
people like You...and Me!

Award winning books by
Shelia E. Bell

Print & Digital
www.sheliawritesbooks.com

Author Shelia E. Bell
God's Amazing Girl

CPSIA information can be obtained
at www.ICGtesting.com
Printed in the USA
LVHW111549010419
612547LV00001B/85/P

9 781944 643119